BRIDE OF THE ROCKIES

QUEEN OF THE ROCKIES, BOOK 5

ANGELA BREIDENBACH

ISBN Ebook: 978-1-957132-04-4

ISBN 13 paperback: 978-1-957132-05-1

ISBN Large Print: 978-1-957132-06-8

Fiction/Historical/Religious

This book is a work of fiction set in a real location. Any reference to historical figures, locations, or events, whether fictional or actual, is a fictional representation. Originally published as Seven Medals and a Bride.

Biblical verses in this book of fiction are taken from Holy Bible, King James Version, KJV, Cambridge, 1769.

Scripture quotations marked (NLT) are taken from the Holy Bible, New Living Translation, copyright © 1996, 2004, 2007 by Tyndale House Foundation. Used by permission of Tyndale House Publishers, Inc., Carol Stream, Illinois 60188. All rights reserved.

Cover Design by Jenneth Dyck.

Published in Missoula, Montana, by Gems Books, an imprint of Gems of Wisdom/ANGELA E BREIDENBACH LLC.

Published in Missoula MT, USA

*Written in admiration for all the women of history whose
shoulders we stand on.*

INTRODUCTION

Though the romance in this historical is fictional, the main characters are surrounded by real people who took part in the Columbian Exposition of 1893. I hope you enjoy reading about all the antics of the women who take it upon themselves to find a wife for a local miner. I giggled a lot writing their matchmaking efforts. I tried really hard to create personalities based on the real people, their notes and quotes in historical documents and newspapers.

The women who forged civilization out of a wilderness in spite of the hardships inspire me. I found a snippet in an antique newspaper that mentioned seven medals won at the 1893 World's Fair. What stopped me and held my fascination wasn't a simple prize at a fair. These women won for their scientific discoveries of new plant life in

Montana. Those discoveries, categorizing, and presentation hit worldwide newspapers making the Montana women's botanical pavilion literally the talk of the world.

Most of these women are named in newspapers, club minutes, and the story-behind-the-story is quite fantastic. They were on a mission and were intense about promoting the beautiful state of Montana. I found a lot of the information and genealogy stored in the Montana Room of the Missoula Public Library in books, on film, and state records.

The newly formed state set aside $100,000 to display the pride and uniqueness of Montana to the rest of the world. The goal was to show how modern the city of Helena was along with how cultured the people, art, and architecture were. They wanted to present their cities as forward-thinking ahead of most cities of the time. This, the people were sure, would bring in more population, tourism, and workers.

The people of Montana were still heavily male who really wanted more women to come. So the politicians allocated $90,000 to the men to present mining, transportation, and the opportunity. And the women? They were given $10,000 to show a few pretty flowers, travel to Chicago, build and furnish a pavilion, and staff that pavilion for 5 months.

Did the women refuse the paltry sum? Not at

all! In fact, these incredible women accepted the challenge, leveled up exponentially, and outshone the men in the mining booth who did not come back with as many awards or their money. Those seven medals the women won were unprecedented. Their scientific exploration had young mothers loading their children in wagons while they drove over all the counties finding new plants never catalogued previously. The women's club bonded over classifying and preserving all those plants in drawings, water color, and dried displays that dwarfed the other states and countries.

Can you imagine loading a passel of children in a wagon for a full day just to find a new flower or weed? Can you imagine any woman doing that for days on end? These women mapped out the counties, assigned women to the areas, and scoured Montana's flora for over a year. I can't imagine what it would be like to put all my six kids in a suburban for a few hours to find a plant. But to do it for a year or more in farm wagons over land that had little for roads and comfortable travel even between farms? I'm in complete admiration.

Come join me in the pages of **Bride of the Rockies** as we see how these women not only stymied the world, but frugally managed their funds, brought home a third of the money allocated along with all the furniture that they used in their pavilion. The money was returned to the state treasury while the furniture was then donated to state buildings and special places. It's still there today almost 130 years later!

Just those facts struck me as being important to preserve. Though this book is a work of fiction, the true history of Helena and Montana are as accurate as humanly possible.

Enjoy!

Angela

BRIDE OF THE ROCKIES

There be three things which are too wonderful for me, yea, four which I know not: The way of an eagle in the air; the way of a serpent upon a rock; the way of a ship in the midst of the sea; and the way of a man with a maid. —
Proverbs 30:18-19

CHAPTER 1

MAY 1, 1893

BETTINA GILBERT GAWKED AT THE WHITE City from a bench on the hurricane deck of the steamship as she balanced a sketchbook on one knee, a white lace glove in her lap to avoid graphite smudges. The clouds clearing from their early morning drapery drew away as if a cord were pulled on a stage revealing the glow of bright white classical structures gleaming in the spring sun. Heaven might as well be laid out before her. The Peristyle's forty-eight Roman columns, one for each US state, and its gateway arches spread the massive colonnade across the park's waterway entrance butted by the mammoth casino on one side and the matching music hall on the other.

From the distance, the shape made by the harbor buildings seemed more like Bettina pictured the Lord's giant throne room, regal and triumphant, calling believers into His presence.

Could she capture that sense of incredible royalty in a sketch before the boat docked? The cacophony of the crowd on board rumbled with unencumbered excitement to discover the Columbian Exposition of 1893. The noise of the crowd on the pier walkway rolled across the short distance to collide with the clamor on the boat as if one hand met the other in wild ovation. Did the angelic chorus sound as loud? God must have rather the regular headache. Bettina pressed lace clad fingertips to her temple.

"Beautiful from this vantage." The expressive awe in the man's words tickled her ears, a calm center in the explosion of buzzing energy. His voice soothed her spirit like the sun on her shoulders eased the shivers after the morning's rainy start. "We're blessed with unusual opportunity."

Against the rising roar from inland, where thousands upon thousands listened to President Cleveland's opening address near the Court of Honor's Columbus fountain, and those on the dock scurried to see the great man press the golden key to open the fair, this man's quiet words subdued Bettina's frayed nerves. "Yes, astonishingly so." She slipped the sketch pencil into her hair and turned into the sun, barely escaping its cloudy curtains, to find her fellow passenger.

Lifting her gloved hand to block the glare, Bettina caught a glimpse of a mustache and dark hair under a bowler as she waited out the signal bell clanging orders to the steamship's crew. Then a woman with several well-dressed children, girls in matching gray frocks and boys in matching gray knickers and vests, jostled into an open space hindering a good view of her congenial companion.

He must have given way—as a gentleman should according to her father. Refreshing since manners seemed sorely lacking as more and more travelers bore down on Chicago the last few weeks. Well, it'd been a pleasant interlude amongst the din. She returned to her sketching.

"Antoine, qu'est-ce que je dis? Votre frère..."

French. Bettina tried to ignore the poor mite's scolding for shoving a sibling, but her love of language and sense of unrequited adventure meant a tiny bit of intentional eavesdropping. Poor bored Antoine was picking on his brothers. She knew exactly what that felt like. Her pencil flew. The boy's face, eyes full of longing, took over the upper corner of her page watching the city from afar.

Who were all these people? What were their home countries like? Why were they here, specifically? She loved digging into the details, but on a much more minute level. The magnitude of the crowds everywhere she looked already drained her people patience. She'd much prefer peeping into a microscope or testing soil samples. But then, she still had to find a way to meet the man she hoped would have a place for her to continue her research. Dr. Kelsey would be here, at the exposition, taking part in the congresses before massive audiences. She couldn't arrive on that day and expect to be prepared. No, coming early to investigate was a wise choice.

She cast a quick, consolation glance at the boy who wanted to be done with the waiting. It had to be harder still to wait when the World's Fair seemed only inches away and as yet so inaccessible. Would anything be as thrilling for him again in his lifetime? Or hers? The boy turned to face away from his family, nose in the air as if watching a seagull, an elbow popped out and jabbed his little brother setting off another squabble. Then he pretended a wide-eyed innocence as his sibling overacted to the injury, sending his mama into another fit of French scolds.

Oh, no. Bettina rolled her lips inward and tightened them to keep from laughing. Anyone could tell what a finger shaking at a nose meant. How many strangers caught her brothers, or her, acting just this way during childhood? She focused on shading dimension into the numerous arches of the Peristyle rather than be an encouraging party to the French lad's mischievous antics. French boys and Irish-American boys. Not so different.

Although she seemed to get away with a few pranks as the middle child to keep her four brothers in line, it was survival as far as she was concerned. Adding an eight-year old sister into the family meant jostling for a new pecking order.

Bettina peeked back at the boy. "I see you." She mouthed at him and signaled between their eyes in case he didn't speak English, he'd understand.

He rewarded her with a knowing grin.

She tipped her pencil to her hat—the silent, secret language of mischievous middles.

His grin grew.

She'd take one-on-one communication any day over parties and crowds. Then she caught sight of another gaze. A little breath wedged in her throat at the handsome stranger's nod of detection. He'd noticed the exchange and joined in the humorous moment. Bettina lowered her lashes and turned toward the dock, a warm blush creeping across her cheeks. She whispered to herself, "No distractions." My, but she liked the confident look of him.

Approaching the already teeming dock doubled the volume and drowned out her ability to think. Today national and international experts began to gather and share scientific discoveries and potential medicines derived from the study of plants. The upcoming congresses promised to educate and entertain on every topic imaginable. Though winning a slot to present her own paper on strategic crop planting for maximum harvest both excited and terrified her. Only the possibility of gaining a position close to home at Oberlin College convinced her parents the summer in Chicago would be worth the sacrifice of letting their daughter go for a short time. But would anyone even want to hear an unknown, let alone a woman botanist, speak on farming techniques? Hopefully one Reverend Doctor F. D. Kelsey and his colleagues. She pushed the anxiety away and concentrated on her plan.

Bettina knew where each one of the featured displays would be housed as well as the illustrious names in botanical science she wanted to meet. She'd gleaned several from research papers at college, and thanks to the detailed articles in the Chicago Tribune for the last year or so, she knew which would be speaking or participating with an exhibit. Sharing her work was less about the audience and more about attracting an expert mentor, preferably the good Reverend Doctor Kelsey, to help her navigate her budding botany career.

The daily speakers in the congresses, where the learned of the world convened to educate and enlighten, held both the key to her future and an example of how she should conduct herself when it came her turn to present. While others took in the sights and exotic experiences like camel rides, Egyptian mummies, and Mr. Ferris' wheel on the specially dubbed Street of Cairo, Bettina intended to expand her horizons professionally by studying the scholars she wished to intern under for an advanced degree. She didn't have time for thrill seeking if the few remaining positions that fit her need for a situation near Cleveland, and her parents, were at stake.

The signal bell clanged its arrival announcement. Closing the sketchpad, she eyed the jam of families, including the French lad still pestering his little brother. The mishmash line flowed out from the stairwell and disappeared down two decks toward departure. That could take a while. A few minutes more to remember the awe-struck moment the White City boardwalk spread like a welcome mat to every nation would be worth the delay disembarking after the mass exodus off the steamboat. But then, she'd visit each botanical and agricultural exhibits first. Of all the places, admiring and studying the leading experts' work at the World's Fair had to be the best opportunity to find a master mentor for a degreed botanist.

Bettina's heart drummed in her ears matching the thrum of the antsy throng. Brilliant minds would walk here this summer. She wanted the chance to meet them, discover unknown species, uses for plant materials, and better ways to manage crops to feed the masses—and one day be considered accomplished among those brilliant minds.

She flipped open the page on her sketchbook again, tucking the loose referral letter from her professor safely in the back pages with her carefully planned list of activities, and tugged the pencil from its mooring under the small purple hat. Flaxen strands floated free of her loose chignon and danced in the breeze over her shoulders as she bent to draft a smart line drawing of her first view from Lake Michigan. Bettina studied the entrancing architecture, ducked again to feather in a little shading for the lagoon, and then shifted on the bench for a better angle to finish the brilliant white, elegant casino left of the pier. The beaux-Art domes on many of the structures seemed similar. She started counting, dipping the end of the pencil as she ticked off each one in sight.

"That's an astounding representation." He leaned over her shoulder blocking the morning sun.

Bettina gasped as she dropped her sketchbook. The blotter slid down her navy skirt and lodged near her boot—until she moved to pick it up at the same time as the ship's paddlewheel chugged, jerking as it reversing direction as it moored alongside the dock. Skittering across the planked decking, still wet from the earlier drizzle, the book careened toward the edge. She stood to give chase.

He shot to the rescue, dropping to a knee and snagging the book by the binding corner before it slid under the boat's rail and over the side. As he rose, the pages blew open and fluttered in the breeze loosing one to float free lifted, lolling on a current.

Her reference letter! "Catch that!" she lurched, arm outstretched, and bumped the handsome stranger into the railing as they both reached for the paper. Her pencil sailed from her fingers and plunged into the waves. She scrambled for a handhold and clutched for the page losing her balance. Her gloved hand slid at the same time as her boot pitching her forward, off her feet, in the direction of lapping water against the hull.

He grasped Bettina around the waist a moment before she tumbled into Lake Michigan three decks below.

She squeaked like a strangled seagull as his saving strength cutoff all airflow.

One arm tight around Bettina, he snagged the errant page from the teasing grasp of the breeze as it blew inward and tipped toward the water as if missing its pencil mate. Setting her back on her feet, he let her loose. "Are you all right?"

Dragging in a deep breath, Bettina clasped the white lace at her throat. "Yes. I don't know what would have happened if you hadn't stopped me." She swallowed as she glanced down at the deep, dark water. "Thank you."

"I'm sorry I caused you such distress during a delightfully peaceful moment in all this hullaballoo." He offered her the page. Miss—" He waited.

Goosebumps erupted as he spoke. "Bettina Gilbert." Was there a nip in the wind?

"Miss Gilbert. I feel I owe you some sort of compensation for damaging your art and for the appalling scare."

The way he said her name with that hint of pleasure in his tone sent little tingles down her spine. "No, please, this is the way I take notes." She meant to make quick eye contact, just to be polite, but that one glimpse led to a smile sparkling in his blue eyes. "I—I'm not an artist." She might not have drowned in the lake but his eyes drew her like a bottomless well. Dark brown, wavy hair refused to maintain the combed back style of the day in the humidity.

"Notes?" Bettina's admirer brought her attention back to the pad as he thumbed to the pencil drawing of the Grecian columns, domes, and spires on the neoclassical architecture. "That's about as creatively detailed a note as I've ever had the pleasure to view. Wait until you see the art on display at the exposition. I've previewed a few in the Manufacturers and Liberal Arts Building. Your notes could rival many of the exhibits."

Coloring, she shook her head. "I appreciate the kind compliment. I've developed the ability to sketch in order to log my studies as a botanist." She shook her head, but a bemused smile touched her lips. "Not an artist." Holding out her hand,

Bettina asked, "May I have my sketchpad back, please?"

Rather than returning it, the man had the gall to take a step away from her. "Might I glance through at a few more?"

"I really wish you wouldn't. Some of my notes are," she paused searching for the right word, "personal. I know it looks like random sketches to you, but those pictures are more like a diary of my thoughts."

His smile disappeared. "My apologies. I meant no intrusion." He gave the scuffed up book back. "Luke Edwards, from Montana. Please to make your acquaintance, though under less than favorable circumstances."

"Pleased to meet you, Mr. Edwards." She gave him a polite nod and shook his outstretched hand with her ungloved one. "I'm sure the circumstances were unavoidable." Sparks tingled in her palm at his touch. She glanced up, back at their clasped hands, and up again. Did he feel the energy, too? Retrieving her hand, she blurted out the first thing that popped into her head. "You don't look like a frontier cowboy." Brilliant observation. Could she take that comment back? "What brings you to the fair?"

"Not everyone in Montana is a cowboy, Miss Gilbert." He pointed to the bench offering to sit with her. "Perhaps you'd let me—" The wind curled its fingers and snatched through his dark hair triumphing in glee as the gust grabbed the bowler off his head and tossed it a goodly distance into ship center. He pivoted to see where it'd blown off to and then back to Bettina, "Pardon me a moment." For a man in a formal suit and starched collar, he dodged nimbly through the shuffling travelers as the boat anchored.

Bettina tried to hold back a grin. But watching the good-looking Montanan dive and resurface amongst the throng reminded her of duck bobbing for fish, albeit unsuccessfully. She shouldn't laugh at his misfortune. But there he was again, bopping up with a hand signal for one more moment. She couldn't help herself. She giggled and pressed her fingers against her mouth. Their eyes connected. For a brief moment, she saw into his heart. Bettina knew something shifted in hers. She lowered her hand to wrap her waist, where he'd held her from disaster and realized she'd lost a glove. Peering around and under the bench, Bettina couldn't find it. She stood to search for her hero. Possibly he'd found it along with his hat? But Mr. Edwards had disappeared in the press of oncoming fair-goers as she was pushed along the ship's railing toward the gangway by the last rush of passengers.

CHAPTER 2

HAT IN HAND, thanks to a quick-acting fellow,
Luke searched for a dark purple velvet hat with
matching ostrich plumes and a white blouse across
the shoulder-to-shoulder sea of humanity moving
off the ship. If he didn't find her now, the possibility of getting to know Miss Bettina Gilbert over
one of those novel carbonated sodas shrank exponentially on the six hundred plus acre grounds.
She'd had a navy blue jacket over her arm to match
her skirt. Possibly she'd donned it?

Straining to see ahead, he slid on a small object
along the wooden deck. Picking it up, the pitifully
dirt-laden lace resembled a rag more than an
expensive ladies accessory. At the very least,
should he find Miss Gilbert, he could gallantly
return her missing glove. Ladies spent a lot of
money on custom gloves. Perhaps she could

salvage the pair by dyeing in tea? Reason enough for pocketing it.

The fact she fascinated him, and wasn't one of the many chosen by his overly helpful self-appointed matchmakers, propelled him to weave in and out of the queue until they closed ranks at the narrow departure point. "Excuse me." He zigged into an opening. "Pardon, if you don't mind." Luke zagged into another break between bodies until he'd made it down both sets of outer stairs.

At the top of the gangway platform, he caught sight of a purple blur bouncing a few feathers at the entrance to the moving walkway. As yet to operate, she skirted the construction with the sway of the crowd—and then, shorter than most, she was gone as if swallowed by a wave. Luke inched forward toward escape from the suffocation of shoulders, umbrellas poking at him, and the heat of so many bodies squashed in too small a space.

On the pier still navigating the narrow board-walk, the crowd parted, thinning at the harbor Peristyle as they accessed the fair's sidewalk system. Surely a proper miss would avoid the casino. But her sketches of the architecture? Maybe she wanted a closer look.

Luke threaded through the massive columns acting as the entrance gate searching up and down the rowed arches. Not a hair. He hightailed it to the highest point of the nearby footbridge spanning the first man-made lagoon, centerpiece for the Court of Honor.

With dozens of people passing over, he stopped and scanned as far through the fair walkways as he could for the enchanting Miss Gilbert and her distinctive purple plumes.

No luck. She'd vanished into the vast opening day masses. Evidently God had other plans in mind for his potential wife, if he planned one at all. Would you mind, Lord, if I—

"Mr. Edwards, did you manage to acquire the chairs?" Mrs. Lydia Fitch asked. The lady's sister lived near downtown Chicago and sold the Montana women antique replacements for two broken pieces of furniture. With the state's contingent working together, though spread throughout several buildings and varying exhibits, he'd agreed to oversee the shipment after the disastrous arrival of a smashed crate. Though why he couldn't meet the ship at the dock escaped him.

In the mass arrivals, he couldn't find a trace of Miss Gilbert while the woman who'd made a top project out of his matrimonial status could find him in a wink. Though only receding thunder from the morning's rainstorm, Luke distinctly felt the heavens laughing. You do have a sense of irony, don't you, Lord?

Luke plastered on a patient smile. "Yes, ma'am, I did. I'll have it offloaded and brought over once the harbor master clears it."

Truth be told, he enjoyed all the fuss the ladies made over him. They'd adopted him as if he were a favored nephew when they learned he wanted to come to Chicago and find a wife. The male to female ratio back home leaned heavily against him regardless of his business success and ownership of both a silver and a copper mine. But a little less zeal wouldn't be amiss. Somehow he hadn't been able to impress the Montana ladies that he was perfectly capable of finding his own wife.

"We do need a respite for weary attendees and a comfortable sitting area for those watching after our work in the pavilion salon."

He chanced another scan of the grounds over her head. Well, not if pretty prospects kept disappearing.

She followed his gaze. "Are you looking for someone in particular or admiring the view?"

He stuck his hands in his pockets and gave his attention to Mrs. Fitch.

Without a hitch, she turned back and continued. "Were you taken with my niece? She's had quite the successful debut." She gave a nonchalant, graceful turn of her wrist gesturing toward the crowd. "The young men are lining up. I'm sure I could put in a good word for you with her parents." She tilted her head conspiratorially to him.

"Uh, I didn't realize—" The very tender girl in question seemed more interested in needlework than discussion. She might be a bit youthful for his twenty-nine years. But then he'd thought the reason for the trip had to do with replacing chairs for the botanical exhibit, not a matrimonial introduction. He surely should have known better where Mrs. Fitch was concerned. He could be convinced to meet the pretty girl again.

Wait. Botanical…botanist…if Miss Gilbert's interests drew her to the Montana flora then he might find her there. Though he had no idea if she came for the day or if she'd return frequently through the summer. Was she even a Chicagoan? Luke's mouth went dry. What if she came from another country? His search could be enormously more difficult.

Mrs. Fitch tapped his elbow. "Would you like me to formally introduce you?"

"Yes." An international bride might take more logistics, but not unreasonable. Wait. Introduce him to whom? He gulped. "What?"

In the few weeks since they'd arrived to set up their agricultural and mining displays, his several supporters were championing his marital opportunities with such fervor that they'd begun a daily habit of scouting every available lady working anywhere nearby. Some aware and some—curiously clueless—to the machinations of his determined "aunts". Evidently the mission was to first determine his interests. They might be more successful if they'd simply listen to him. He liked a strong personality who knew her mind. Any other might not be prepared for his home further out on the range than in the city. Helena was very modern, but he wouldn't have the miracle of electricity for a while yet regardless of owning a copper mine. His self-appointed matchmakers had their own ideas of what a perfect counterpart looked like and so far it hadn't yet agreed with his. Was he searching for the impossible?

"I'll invite Janey to see one of your talks."

The Mines and Mining building should have been far enough away from the Woman's Building to deter such regular romps through his day, but they had him outnumbered. It almost seemed as if they had assigned shifts. "But—"

"You can tell her all about our silver Lady Justice statue. Just leave out the part that she's modeled after that hussy actress from New York, will you? Why they couldn't use one of our lovely Montana ladies as the model." She shook her head, then brightened at her decision. "Yes, that'll be a good start."

"Mrs. Fitch—" If they hadn't been frenzied enough, opening day seemed to set off a race to be the lady that found Luke Edwards a wife almost as important as whether they'd out-win the men in medals.

"No, no need to thank me. We promised to bring home a bride for you and that's what we'll do."

He stopped searching the distance and turned

to look at his doting friend. Was there a competition going on? If he didn't find one first, he might be trampled by the sweetest, most good-intentioned cupids in the process with Mrs. Fitch, Mrs. Moore, and Mrs. McAdow in a three-way tie for the lead. Who said women weren't competitive?

"You know it'd be so lovely to have family around. You might be quite taken with Janey once you get to know the little angel. She's quite talented and would make quite the perfect wife for a success-oriented young man like yourself, if you're looking for a smart match. You are truly looking for an accomplished homemaker, aren't you?" She didn't seem to breathe between sentences. The opposite of her shy niece.

Quiet. Contemplative. That personality might do well with his, but he still needed to feel an attraction. The moment or two he waited in the sunroom with her could hardly tell the full story. Neither had been aware the meeting was contrived for their benefit. At least he didn't.

"I've heard of young men sowing their wild oats. I'm sure that's not you. Though you haven't really shown much interest in the few you've met thus far. Janey now, she's quite a girl, don't you think?"

He couldn't help it, the word seemed to have been planted in his skull. "Quite." He nodded. "Mrs. Fitch, you haven't set up a contest between you all?"

"A contest? Why, what foolishness. No, the only contest I know of is to see who gets more medals, the men or the women." She tapped his arm with her folded fan. "That wouldn't be happening either if those lummox's hadn't crowed they'd bring home the most and only given us ten percent of the budget. And how is that going, Mr. Edwards?"

A tiny purple spec caught his attention in the distance against the backdrop of a white wall like an iris rising from a late winter snow. Luke squinted against the bright sunshine. How had she managed to get that far ahead?

At this point, he had a choice to make. Let go of the first girl who'd captured his interest in seconds or indulge his curiosity about the adorably humble botanist-not-artist with olive green eyes, shapely figure, and the prettiest smile he'd ever seen. "Mrs. Fitch, would you excuse me?"

"Certainly." Her words trailed behind him. "Shall I see you with the chairs—"

"Yes, this afternoon sometime. If you'll excuse me." He dashed north, in the direction of the state buildings. "Miss Gilbert! Bettina Gilbert!"

CHAPTER 3

Bettina toured several state manors filled to the brim with displays of every kind touting their local prides and products before entering the exhibits in the Woman's Building. The incredible size of this one building could easily take her the day if she gave each pavilion its due.

Talented women around the country shared their art, inventions, and business endeavors. Basics like clothing design, gardening, and canning had a spot as well. With daily awards during the exposition, a jar of peaches, the batch judged on color and flavor, already had it's pretty blue ribbon proudly placed center front in Georgia's booth. But corn and wheat throughout the cavernous struc-ture held the most ground from states like Illinois, Iowa, and Nebraska.

A few new growth records intrigued her, as did

the achievements hanging on walls and in specially built presentations kiosks. Every so often, she sketched ideas to reference in her talk during the congresses next month. When had the world birthed innovation any more than now? She hadn't even been inside the largest building Mr. Edwards mentioned.

His fine-looking face sprang to mind and she scanned the area. Silly. She'd met him all of twice in the space of an hour. It would take a week to explore those exhibits she'd planned to see, let alone all those not on her list. A man was not on her list. Even one as extraordinarily heroic and handsome as Mr. Luke Edwards.

Bettina straightened her shoulders and continued through the building's magnificent offerings. She rounded another corner and took in the beautifully designed scientific botanical display the Chicago Tribune publicized as being created with precise classifications by the Montana women and a "not-to-miss" exhibit. Did he work this huge stall? A building inside a building, more accurately. Bettina slowed her pace and searched the faces around the area as well as inside the display salon.

Montana's new botanical discoveries proved fascinating. Ten frames hung on an immense carved and polished wood pillar, books filled with seeds and pressed flora lounged on stands, and some on a highly polished table. Braided grain stalks and weavings covered the pavilion walls. The assortment of pinecones and the decorative arrangement showed the skill of florists as well as interior designers. Another ten frames of beautifully preserved wildflower bouquets, card noting Emil Starz as the preparer, fashioned an impressive visual of the variety and scope found in the mountainous region. She wanted to see this wild country in person.

Blue eyes and dark hair flashed into her thoughts yet again. If only he knew how often in the last few hours she'd been disappointed not to find him in the crowd. Statistically speaking, an irrational hope. Though didn't the statistics rise around his home state exhibits? How had a chance meeting taken over her mental processes? She blinked rapidly. Her parents would never approve.

Bettina touched the edge of a book to admire the seed to flowering phases, pressed and pinned in order of each stage as recorded by a Mrs. Jennie Moore. Every entry in perfect systematic order from kingdom to species, just as the article foretold. An occasional watercolor recorded a shrub or a leaf on a page representing a plant too large to put in the book.

Unlike much of the vegetation in Illinois and the surrounding states, she'd not encountered several of the Rocky Mountain species before. The small *Lewisia Rediviva* known informally as the bitterroot flower was not only beautiful, but edible? She filed that tidbit into her journal with a quick line drawing and notation. How wonderful to walk among the fresh discoveries of the frontier. Probably the closest she'd get knowing Mama's feelings on how far Chicago was from Cleveland already.

"You would think he was smitten!" One well-dressed woman said to a small nearby group. They all wore matching black skirts and ornately embroidered white blouses with ruffled high-neck collars. A banner, in the colors of the new state flag, draped each shoulder down to the hip. The embroidery spelled out in yellow-gold thread the state name. The Montana women aimed to impress and were doing a good job of it, too, in their opening day finery.

She perused the woven wall hangings, inhaling the earthy scent of grain and the various grasses, to avoid interrupting the conversation at the edge of the pavilion. The decorative presentation kept Bettina's mind wrestling with the longing to see it all in its natural habitat—until snippets of the nearby chat showered her with accidental gossip.

"Lydia, he hasn't show a bit of interest in any particular girl yet. None of us has uncovered the most likely candidate. Your Janey still has as much chance of landing him as any other girl at this point than an acquaintance."

"I do believe I heard him calling out to a Miss Gert or Bert...possibly Stuart." She tapped a gloved finger against her cheek. "I'm sure I heard the name

Serena. What do you suppose running after someone like that would mean otherwise? He's smitten, I tell you." She waggled that gloved finger at her friends. "Ladies, your duty to our poor, single Mr. Edwards is to find this Serena Stuart. His happiness may depend on it."

Oh dear, that poor Mr. Edwards would find himself married soon, whether he liked it or not, if these ladies had their way. He was both charming and heroic. Bettina touched her hand to her waist. Whoever he chose would be a fortunate girl.

Lydia nodded. "Yes, that's the name. I'm sure of it. Though it makes me heartbroken that Janey may get passed over by such an eligible bachelor. She's quite a catch, you know, for any of our Helena millionaires. He'd be a lucky man to have her."

"They'd make a lovely couple." Another woman agreed.

Bettina snuck a quick glance at Lydia. She seemed genuinely disappointed her niece hadn't yet impressed this revered saint of a man. Mr. Edwards appeared to have earned admiration from those that knew him well—and one who didn't, if she admitted the truth.

Several other ladies, evidently friends, bobbed their heads in agreement while tsk-tsking Mr. Edwards lack of taste.

One said, "We'll simply have to help him see her virtues so he doesn't dismiss her lightly. But our promise is to help Mr. Edwards come home with a bride by the end of summer." Her voice dripped with warning. "I would truly hate to fail such a wonderful man after we all agreed to help. If I were only twenty years younger."

They all giggled with her.

"Jennie, you're right." Lydia responded with a sorrowful sigh. "Though, it's our duty we must help him be sure of his choice. Don't you think I should still invite my niece to come down? He couldn't have had much time to meet her. Though I had sent ahead and made sure my sister knew of the prospect. I do so want family near, if there's a chance."

The smile slipped across Bettina's lips. The ladies seemed so invested in their matchmaking project even if one or two had ulterior motives. She'd heard men outnumbered women in that fledgling state.

An idea struck. If her parents wanted her safely married to a bright, successful man, she could always use Montana's need for women as a suggestion. It might put a damper on the belief their daughter should only work until children arrived. Though she'd have a hard time keeping a straight face if she declared she was moving to Montana to have her pick of husbands. They knew she'd never dare move so far away, not after all they'd given her. Loyalty was such a small thing to give back to those who loved her wholeheartedly without expectation of repayment. But, what if it helped stave off the constant conversations about marriage. Maybe. She'd think about it.

Bettina put her hands behind her then remembered the missing glove. Her mother was a stickler for observing social custom. Tucking her bare hand into the pocket of her walking skirt, Bettina focused full attention to the lines of the grain weaving, so as not to be rude, and cleared her throat. She shouldn't be listening to what didn't concern her. But her thoughts squiggled back like doodles on her sketchpad. So the man from Montana was already sweet on a gal. A little pang of disappointment hit her. She'd have liked to— what did it matter? If not that girl, his cherubic matchmakers had another in mind already. Did he have days or weeks until ignorance changed to wedded bliss? She had no doubt these Montana ladies meant to take home as many winning medals as possible and a bride for Mr. Luke Edwards.

How romantic to find a sweetheart at the Columbian Exhibition. Wouldn't that make a grand story for future generations? The world to choose from and two lovers find the one in all the earth meant for—it wouldn't be her story. Not yet, anyway. Although, at the rate these ladies wanted to interfere, it may not be his either. She choked back a giggle, pretending a light cough, as several other visitors filled in around her.

"Lydia, we've been remiss." One of the ladies

pointed to the gathering fair attendees perusing their pavilion. "We have visitors."

"Hello," one of the women approached Bettina, "my name is Jennie Moore." She offered a handshake. "This is Mrs. Lydia Fitch and Mrs. J.E. Light. This exhibit has been completely created and designed by the women of Montana." The loving pride of both their handiwork and home state glowed all over them.

"Goodness," Bettina answered Jennie while selecting the page she read about the bitterroot flower, "you're the one who catalogued all these specimens so well."

Mrs. Moore nodded, a little flushed with pleasure at the compliment. "That one, the bitterroot, is a favorite of my friend, Mrs. Mary Long Alderson of Bozeman. She's nominating it for our state floral emblem, though it may take awhile to happen."

"It would be a worthy choice. I believe I've noticed each of your names on the cards here and there." And I may have overheard your conversation. "What an honor to meet all of you ladies." She shook hands around the small circle. "I'm Bettina Gilbert."

"What questions do you have about our great state of Montana or the vegetation there?"

"As a botanist—"

"Did you hear that, ladies?" Mary announced, "She's a botanist."

The surprise drew the them all together.

She blushed at the attention. "Thank you. I'm impressed with the care given to the science, including the sequence. But the beauty of your display is something to behold." She splayed her hand toward the enormous rows of braided grain stalks climbing the pillars holding up the gazebo-styled cross-slat roofing.

"Oh, that means so much to us, dear." Mrs. Moore beamed. "We've been working on this since they announced the White City would be built. Dozens of us collected specimens from all over the state. One of our ladies even rode around the range toting her children in a wagon searching for seeds and specimens not yet discovered. She went farm to farm and town to town where the trains couldn't go."

"That's very much what I want to do—discover!" Bettina's passion for the topic flared. "I'm hoping to work for the new head of Oberlin's botany department. I'd like to integrate what I've learned in college to applied use—determine how to really help people with my abilities." Images from her childhood, of dirty street water tainted by sewage and very little food clamored in her head with the memory of not being allowed to kiss the cheek of she who birthed her. To say goodbye as she died in filthy rags, on a dirty mattress, in a room that stank of piled up waste. Then she was gone from the pneumonia that chased typhoid all too commonly, the good doctor said. In all that grief and pain, Bettina remembered intense hunger cramping her belly. A feeling she hadn't ever forgotten. That and the odors of garbage, sour breath, and death.

"Clara should take her under her wing." Mrs. Fitch suggested.

"Lydia has worked tirelessly to produce seven hundred specimens here while our friend Clara McAdow—oh, there she is now." Jennie Moore waved at her friend across the wide aisle. "Yoo-hoo, Clara, come meet this lovely gal." She continued extolling Mrs. McAdow's contributions. "Now Clara has worked on another display in the Horti-culture Building, but she rubs elbows with the likes of Reverend F. D. Kelsey. I believe he's the one at Oberlin?" She waited for Bettina's agreement.

They knew him? Maybe Montana wasn't the far frontier. "Yes," she nodded. "I've read his work, but not yet had the pleasure to meet such an esteemed scientist. It's his department I've applied to. But the referral letter from my professor didn't arrive until just this week. I brought it with me hoping for the chance to pass it to him in person."

"We'll get you introduced properly then, shall we?"

Mrs. Fitch enthusiastically added, "Who knows where that association may lead? I imagine assis-tants for his department are chosen from those he knows, don't you?"

Besides scientific interests, it seemed the

Montana ladies had a talent for being well connected in society regardless of their distant homes. The world seemed a little smaller all of a sudden. Thank you, Lord! But what could she offer these mavens in return?

Clara joined the growing circle as the passersby ebbed. The others buzzed at her like bees dancing with the hive queen and filling in what she'd missed. "You'll enjoy Reverend Kelsey. He has such a quick mind for Latin, being well versed in the language through his theological education. His mind snaps through the genus and species as if he's conversing with friends at a dinner party. But then everyone is his friend."

She turned to the group as a whole. "We're in the running for another medal for our scientific botanical display! I heard the judges debating over there at the Iowa booth."

"That would make seven!" Mrs. Fitch clapped her hands. "Now what will those men say when we mount those awards for all to see!"

"I don't know that we can beat that Iowa display though." Jennie leaned against the table edge, hands bracing beside her hips for balance. "Did you see how many ways they managed to decorate with corn? Really, right down to rosettes out of husks. Though Colorado isn't going to do well with those heavy frames sagging off their pillar."

"Of all the displays that shouldn't win, I think that man from Ireland claiming no good oatmeal could be made in America. Can you imagine the gall?" Mrs. Fitch plunked her fists at her ample waist and shook her head.

"Well then, our prairie farmers will just have to grow heavier oats." Jennie Moore's eyes twinkled as she tossed her head with a little snap punctuating her words. "But first we women need to take home more awards than our men. They're edging up on us with the mining and minerals."

"You don't think they're serious, do you?" Bettina tilted her head a tad and scrunched her nose. "A mining display is so different from a scientific botanical display."

"If those coffee slurping, backslapping men think they can breeze in here and insult our efforts then why not beat them and show those cowboys what we can do?" Mrs. McAdow pointed her finger all around the group, but her grin betrayed her. "You all heard it. Do we put up with that or do we stand up for all womankind?"

Mrs. Fitch lamented with her. "We wouldn't even have competition from Nevada if Idaho's display hadn't burned on that train. Is it wrong to wish they'd made it? How fair is it that Nevada couldn't plan far enough in advance to buy a space and then slides in at Idaho's misfortune?"

In the space of thirty minutes, well over a dozen Montana women hobnobbed about their plant studies, specimens, and chances for exposition medals.

Bettina had a sense of belonging in the camaraderie, though the women had varying levels of involvement for most it was more about advancing Montana's natural resources and establishing the state's emergence into the national marketplace. The common goals, scientific language, understanding of the world around her, and undeniably passionate interest in the botanical life God created burst from her like a crocus waking in winter snow. Even the merriment of a good-natured race against the men made her comfortable.

Bettina mentally counted around the circle wanting to pinch herself. A dozen women talking her language, save her mother's circle of gardening friends, and not about whose blooms were the prettiest. The beauty of flowers, notwithstanding, her fascination lay in the elegance of God's infinite design and how to best steward it to help her fellow man. "I want to believe it's possible to find a solution to the poverty and hunger in our nation. What if we could cultivate at higher yields or find new varieties of plant nourishment like your *Lewisia Rediviva?*"

For a girl who didn't socialize much outside of her studies the last few years, Bettina couldn't stop from asking more questions if she tried. "Mrs. Moore, I noticed the bitterroot is designated as edible and the Indians believe it has some sort of medicinal value. Can we develop that into sustainable crops? Are there other Montana plants that grow naturally that might be helpful this way or grow in other locales? Are there great expanses of land rich enough for farming?"

"You do have an inquisitive mind and a good heart. Bettina, is it?"

"Yes, Mrs. Moore," she nodded. "I hope to find answers for those questions. Answers that will make a difference in the lives around us. What if these new discoveries eradicated typhoid?" Still too common and rampant in Chicago even fourteen years after—she shivered away the image of a woman dying and brushed away the memory of tears on a cheek. She couldn't focus on the future if she lived in the pain of her past. "May I reference your work in my upcoming talk?"

"You may." Mrs. Moore leaned in and grasped Bettina's hand. "And call me Jennie, please. Together," she motioned to the group, "we'll see what we can do to help you. But you simply must consider coming to Montana."

Did she just wink at the other ladies?

"It'll be a great pleasure to get to know you while we're here." She looked around the circle of women. "Wouldn't that be something you'd all like to do as well?"

At their wholehearted agreement, Jennie added, "It's much better to have many different perspectives than to rely on only *one* acquaintance."

Mrs. Fitch nodded. "Call me Lydia. It's settled

then. Come spend time with us here at our exhibit. We could use a knowledgeable volunteer."

She couldn't afford not to accept. These maven matchmakers had a penchant for connecting people. And she needed connections in her field to get one of the few positions at Oberlin or another university that would gain her access to grants and permissions for studies. That's all they meant, right?

"Miss Gilbert?" Luke Edwards rolled in a cart with several carved wooden chairs on it—and one no longer truant black bowler on his head.

Jennie's rounded eyes couldn't look more surprised than Bettina's—or Lydia's. The rest of the gathered group tossed meaningful glances like popcorn.

"Gilbert." Lydia burst out. "Yes, I suppose that's what I heard earlier."

Definitely not the kind of connection Bettina wanted the Montana women to focus on for her. O-h-h. Is that what Jennie's invitation to Montana was about? Bettina wanted career, not romantic associations. What if these ladies all thought her purpose was husband hunting? No, no, no. Better to extricate herself as quickly as possible and keep her prospects professional. "Mr. Edwards, good to see you found your errant hat. Nice to see you again."

"O-o-o-h." Said the three cupids collectively

drawing out the word like an angelic chorus, and then looking one to another.

"I did. A gentleman caught it for me near the stairwell. I also found your, er..." he noticed the odd looks from his doting supporters. He cleared his throat and pulled something from his vest pocket nearest his heart. "...glove." Without taking his eyes off of the trio, as if keeping them in check, he handed over the heavily stained accessory. "Although, I think my hat fared better."

"O-o-h." They sang in whispered unison while gaping at the heavily stomped, no longer white, lace glove. The other ladies that hadn't been present for the earlier conversation in the pavilion expressed a range of confusion.

"I'm sorry for the condition," he added, "further aggravated by my own shoe, I'm sure."

She took the soiled glove and smiled through her discomfort at being the center of attention again. Especially this kind of attention. She darted a glance at the ladies she'd been so at home with moments before.

"I do hope it can be salvaged."

A sage nod accompanied by a long look between Lydia and Jennie drew Mrs. Light's attention to the situation as she returned to the group. Lydia made a tiny head tip toward Luke Edwards and then Bettina. Mrs. Light responded with a slow nod in silent in understanding, as did the rest of the circle.

Was everyone in on the matrimonial prospects of Mr. Luke Edwards? And they thought she might be one? Heat crept up Bettina's collar. The vaulted ceiling that seemed a mile above earlier suddenly closed in on her. "I'm sure it'll be fine. Though I've felt quite awkward with only one since." She held up both hands and shrugged. "What can a girl do when she's away from home? I best find another pair. Well, again, thank you." She stepped backward.

He stepped forward, waltzing into her retreat as Luke cupped her elbow. "I tried to catch you outside the steamboat but you'd gotten too far ahead of me."

If Luke Edwards was sweet on someone he chased from the steamboat, that meant—No! The hot flush stole up from her throat into her cheeks.

Then he offered another, more tangible surprise. An elongated, elegant, but very thin box tied with a purple satin ribbon. "I picked these up at the Spanish fashion counter to ease your distress. I used yours to match the size. I hope they'll fit."

He replaced her gloves? Such a costly gesture and an unnecessary one. "I couldn't, Mr. Edwards, but thank you."

"Oh, what a shame. I suppose that means you don't accept my apology." He looked crestfallen.

The circle of women gaped, first at the pretty box and then to Luke Edwards and then halting on

Bettina, all in synch as if a string passed before a row of kittens. Their eyes fastened on her watching, waiting. Would they pounce to protect their favored son?

"Of course." She rushed to soothe the group as well as the man. "Of course I accept your, uh, apology. I simply meant your gift is too—"

"Small?"

Their personal audience gasped, audibly and again in unison.

Panic fluttered in Bettina's stomach. She'd never experienced a gift so thoughtful—and romantic—at the same time as fear so palpable that she'd make a misstep.

He untied the ribbon and opened the box revealing delicate Spanish lace fit for a much more elegant lady than she could ever hope to be. "I'll search for another until you are satisfied if these aren't to your liking."

"No, please." She touched the beautiful paper, almost afraid to lift the precious gift. "They're truly lovely."

"Not as lovely as the woman whose art I ruined and glove I stained under my shoe. Will you accept?" He gave her a questioning smile. "I do hope to be in your good graces here forward."

"I, uh, yes." Her lips parted as she gazed into his shining eyes and took the box. "Thank you." She backed away. "Ladies, it's been a delight. I hope to see you again."

"Wait!"

"Yes, Mr. Edwards?"

He tugged at his collar. He raised his eyebrows expectantly at his champions. "Ladies, could you excuse us please?" If there were a little heavier emphasis on "please", Bettina couldn't fault him.

"Of course, dear," Lydia patted his arm. "We'll just, uh," she looked around. "We've other business to discuss." They scattered around the pavilion salon talking amongst themselves.

"Miss Gilbert, would you do me the honor of allowing me to buy you one of those refreshing sodas?"

"A soda?" She did feel thirsty. But he'd already spent so much on the gloves. How could she possibly allow him to—

She caught an interested peep or two darting over a shoulder here and there. Then a not so quiet whisper, "Could she be the one?"

"Do you think?"

"He hasn't shown such passionate interest...."

"Shush, they'll hear us."

Bettina's face burned. If she turned his invitation down, would she insult him and ruin her budding opportunity with the Montana women?

"No expectation except that I'd like to enjoy your company for a few minutes." He closed the distance between them keeping his smiling eyes on hers. "I'd be honored if you'd accept." He thumbed back over his shoulder. "And I think they're rooting for me."

What could she say? "I—" If he worked with everyone, he'd know soon enough they'd invited her to volunteer this summer and that she'd accepted. Might as well be on good terms with Luke Edwards, too. The problem was good terms with Luke Edwards could easily become something more if the uneven patter of her heart were a sign. Or the weakness in her knees that grew as he came closer. Or the fact that she loved the timbre of his voice.

"Unless, of course, another day would be more convenient. I wouldn't want to impose on any plans you might have already."

No one pretended to be talking any more. Tiny nods of encouragement and a flutter of fingers from Lydia Fitch telling her to go with him.

She inclined her head. "I am a bit thirsty," she saw Jennie's nod telling her to accept, "for a soda."

A small sigh from a dozen women, let out at the same time, resembled the sound of rustling leaves through the rafters.

CHAPTER 4

"Have you heard of candied popcorn?"
Luke pointed at the busy booth on the thorough-
fare. An ornate sign advertised *A Cracker Jack, Sweet
confection of popcorn with peanuts and molasses invented
by Frederick William Rueckheim and Brother*. The aroma
of buttery popcorn and rich molasses wafted over
to them floating in the warm, late spring air. His
mouth watered at the scent.

Bettina indulged his sudden curiosity. "Cracker
Jack. Yes, it's delicious. Would you like to taste it?"
Slipping her hand through his elbow, she tugged
him along as she shared what she knew. "There's a
little shop that started selling earlier this year near
where I live. It's fun to get some and share it
during readings, picnics, and parties."

They parked themselves at the back of the long
line. "That good?"

"Sweet chewy popcorn and peanuts in a candy sauce? Delectable." She craned to see the front of the line. "I wish it wasn't so sticky, but I can't resist."

"Then I'm sure I won't be able to either." He didn't mean the Cracker Jack stand as he looked at her.

When Bettina glanced up, her green eyes caught the light. All he could do was stare.

Then she asked him to put words together coherently. "Why don't you tell me a little about yourself? Until today, the only thing I knew about Montana and its people is that they became a state four years ago. That's not very long to become civilized. I'm so curious." She shrugged with a half smile. "Well, and I now know much more about the flora from visiting your exhibit."

"You realize there's more than one Montana exhibit? We're a diverse population for as few of us as there are."

"I haven't been as far around the fair as I'd have liked today." She turned her head to look around and lifted a shoulder slightly. "The sheer size of it is daunting. I've been able to take in several agricultural and botanical displays. But I didn't look for any particular state presentations, other than a quick walk through a few buildings." She admitted.

"Why did you come, if not to experience the world at your fingertips?"

"I came to connect with botanists more than anything." She looked to see how the line was moving. "What other exhibits should I see when I come back?"

She planned to come back! What would she enjoy? "There's the Montana Building full of crafts and skilled workmanship. You'll learn our state has talents and resources that rival any in the known world. We're much more civilized than you think."

She giggled at his twitching lips. "That sounds like an interesting exhibit. What else?"

The mining exhibits would likely fascinate the scientist in Miss Gilbert, but Luke was after the opportunity to properly court her, if she wasn't already spoken for. If she believed Montana offered civility and culture, there'd be one less hurdle to leap should she consider him husband material. "Then this evening one of our ladies will sing at the opening of the music hall." He decided to take a chance. "Do you like music?"

"Yes." She moved forward with him in the line. "But we're supposed to be talking about you."

"I like music."

She laughed and his heart pounded a little harder. A wife with a gentle, but quick laugh. Yes, that would be a good quality. Humor could help weather hard times.

"What kind of music do you like?"

"All kinds."

"Ah, too general I'm afraid. Please be more specific."

More specific? That answer would satisfy most women. Could that mean true interest? He thought for a moment. "I suppose I enjoy marches that inspire and invigorate, like John Phillips Souza, and songs with words."

She looked a little surprised. "Songs with words?"

"Songs I can sing when I'm working or want to take my mind off something difficult."

"Oh, that's interesting." She considered his answer. "Then you like to sing as well. See? I learned something about you. Music is cultivated so therefore," she paused and gave him a mischievous look down her nose, "I declare thou must be civilized."

Her playful expression made him smile. "We Montanans are relatively sophisticated, Miss Gilbert. We're even a cultured people. I'd be happy to prove it if I may escort you to the concert tonight?"

She grinned, but shook her head. "I do appreciate your thoughtful invitation. But I've promised to return home before dark. My parents are worried enough that I'm off alone."

She's from Chicago. "How did you manage to pull off such a feat then?"

"I explained the need to make connections with people I admire in my field. It's not appropriate to take parents along for potential business contacts."

"Wise on both sides." They finally reached the cart and she waited while he ordered. Hands full of a box loaded with fresh caramel corn, peanuts sprinkled through it, Luke guided Bettina to the soda shop and managed to order sandwiches and sparkling refreshments in half the time it took to obtain the sweets. They found a shady spot next to a tree surrounded by droves of fair-goers picnicking or resting on the lawn and a duck quacking in the pond.

"All right, your turn. What interested you in botany?" He asked then separated a chunk of sticky stuff from the rest. He leaned back against the tree and chewed a bite as he listened, amused at the delicate way she handled the candied corn. Neither had chosen the sandwiches first.

"When my oldest brother began studying medicine, my father bought a microscope. I thought it was the most fascinating toy ever. I put everything I could find under it. Plant life fast became my favorite." She picked a blade of grass. "Did you know you can see leaves breathe under a microscope? Actually, they're undergoing photosynthesis and creating oxygen so we can breathe. But the way light becomes food in, say, a blade of grass is amazing." She spun it between her thumb and forefinger. "Don't you think?"

He thought he understood. "Where I see a

blade of grass, you see a whole different world. Is that it?"

"Yes." Bettina tilted her head. "But it's more. I see ideas, solutions to many of the problems our world faces like starvation, healing, and even future inventions. Can you imagine what it would be like to discover a way to optimize crops for higher production? How many more people could we feed if crops produced even ten percent more? Lack of nutrition is the highest cause of illness and mortality. What if a new plant enzyme cured a childhood disease? Who's going to cure tuber-culosis?"

"You see all that in a plant?" His brows drew close. "What do you see when you look at an animal then? Or a human being?"

She peeked up from under the short brim of her pretty purple hat. "Complex. Human nature is part of that package."

He chuckled. The woman before him could be described as that and then some. "How does one study the complexities of human nature?"

She dipped her chin and brushed her fingers across the grass.

He couldn't see her face except for the gentle slope of her cheek and the length of her graceful neck. His fingers itched to brush her soft skin the way she touched the lawn.

"I don't know. That's why I chose plants." Then she raised her face to him. "I've never been very comfortable with people. At school," she gestured back toward the Woman's Building, "and with people who enjoy the science of botany, I know how to communicate. But I'm less of a social person than most. I don't understand how to—"

What was it about this woman that made him want to encourage her? "You're doing fine with me." Very fine, as a matter of fact. He doubted the conversation would be as stimulating with her if all she wanted to discuss were dresses, shopping, and gossip. "I've never thought of a blade of grass or a leaf breathing or making oxygen so I could breathe. You look at creation differently than anyone I've met before."

Bettina grimaced. "I know. Again, I don't know how to make small talk no matter how hard I try. Hence my mother fears I'll never marry." She shrugged.

"No beau then?"

"No."

Not spoken for. If he could leap for joy at the news, he would. He checked his excitement so as not to push her away. He might be on a time schedule with only these few months, but she didn't need to know it. "I take it that's not on your favorite topics list either?"

"Marriage isn't a bad topic. I just don't know of many men that want a woman who wants to work after the wedding." She repositioned her legs, curling them on the other side. "My father says most men aren't enthused about a woman driving the cart at full speed. But I'm not ready to hand over the reins and darn socks. I like the challenge of accomplishment."

The curve of her hip drew his fascination as she moved into a more comfortable position. He needed a wife and quick! But he didn't want only that. The miners who'd met and married their mail-order brides in one day didn't always have the happiest homes. He'd watched too many disastrous examples, even abandonment because they couldn't work things out. He knew of a few miners that worked and lived at their stakes, beautiful wives at home, avoiding married life after spending so much money to bring a wife to Montana.

He didn't fear marriage. But he sure feared being in the wrong marriage. Slow it down and get the right wife, his father had said. Get to know her first. Wasn't that what he was trying to do?

He swallowed and put his mind back on her words. "So you're not ruling out marriage, if the right fellow came along?"

"No. I look forward to finding the right fellow, as you say. I just don't think he's going to be all that easy to find. They all seem to want wives who dress pretty and pop out lots of pretty babies." She clasped a hand over her mouth. Her eyes widened and her face flared a peachy pink.

Luke reached out and tugged her fingers away brushing her lips with his thumb. "Please don't be embarrassed with me. Not all men want that kind of wife. Makes for dull evenings if there's nothing to talk about, don't you agree?" He held her fingers loosely entwined between them in the grass. "People need to find common ground and know they have interests to share before picking a mate." Would she pull away?

She didn't immediately. Bettina offered a smile and slow nod, though she lowered her eyes again as her face cooled. "Ah, but I think you have your own matchmaking dynasty back there." Dusty brown lashes hid her thoughts. "I'm not so sure you are going to get a chance to choose your wife. Are you?"

He shook his head. "I'm sorry if they embarrassed you. They mean well. I've told them all this is something a man has to do on himself. I don't think they believe me though." He gave her a wry grin. "Some of us are looking for a smart wife who makes a man think and can hold her own. Montana is a place that needs men and women who want to develop her resources. There's opportunity to create the future there for goal-minded people." Releasing her hand, he leaned in and touched her chin willing her to lift her gaze to his. When she did, he added, "Some of us are intrigued by women who have goals and dreams."

Her green eyes illuminated. "Oh."

"But hopefully she won't rule out children." Luke half-teased.

Her face relaxed into a bright smile. "A woman like that might be convinced." She rose to her knees. "I really need to be going. We're staying in a townhouse in the city this summer. The omnibus schedule should get me home before dark, if I hurry."

"I'll see you to the stop." He stood offering a hand to help her rise.

She accepted. Then as she brushed grass from her skirt, he picked up the residue of their late lunch. Luke deposited the empty box and cups in the receptacle as an exotically dressed runner with a wicker seat on wheels attached to long handles approached. "It's a long walk. Would you mind a rickshaw to the gate?"

"Delighted."

He signaled the driver. "Front gate, nearest the downtown omnibus stop, please."

Luke guided her into the wicker seat basket.

Once settled, she said, "I've traveled by steamship in, and now rickshaw out. Today has been an adventure the whole way through."

He climbed in beside Bettina.

The runner raised the long wooden bars to his hips and headed toward the main gate, city side. A short ride later he collected a few coins from Luke and set off after another fare.

"When will you return?"

"I haven't a set schedule, but I did agree to volunteer at the Montana pavilion with you and your friends. I suppose I should stop in tomorrow morning to set a schedule?"

"I'll let the ladies know to expect you." He'd find a reason to visit, often.

The horses clopped to a stop drawing the long carriage to a halt. Ten to twelve passengers filed down the three wooden steps. Very few looked to be leaving on this omnibus. With concerts at several points and hours left for the midway to run yet, the transportation system would be heavily taxed a few hours from now.

"What do you actually do at the exhibit? I mean besides buying candied corn and entertaining tourists?" She asked with a light tone.

"I don't work at that exhibit, Miss Gilbert." He took her hand to assist with boarding the rear steps into the long carriage. "My purpose here is to promote the mineral, ore, and mining industry of Montana to the world."

She stared at him. "You're a miner?"

"Yes and no. I'm a mine owner looking for opportunities to grow and attract business from the resources in my state. And I admit that I hope to find a wife who would enjoy doing those things with me." He squeezed her fingers. "I'll be looking forward to seeing you again."

She snatched back her hand. "It was nice meeting you, Mr. Edwards. Thank you for a lovely afternoon. I don't think we have those commonalities you're looking for."

Had he offended her by being honest? "Miss Gilbert?"

She disappeared into the omnibus.

What just happened? He stared after the departing vehicle taking away the one woman he wanted.

CHAPTER 5

THE MONTH of May had passed into a lovely June. The flowers and trees burst colorful beauty all over the carefully planned grounds.

Bettina volunteered two to three days a week though she remained cautious around Luke Edwards. Getting involved with someone so far from her ideology would be a disaster. Her personal feelings about mining notwithstanding, how could she compromise? After all, his goals cost lives while hers were to save them.

But, oh my. My, my, my how she liked his magnanimous personality. His low laugh that sent ripples through her belly. She admired the confidence in his walk and the breadth of his shoulders.

With the Mining and Mineral Building at a distance, it hadn't been too hard to keep space between she and Luke as well. But she couldn't seem to take her eyes off him when he arrived with supplies or to assist one of the other ladies. Unfortunately, Lydia or Jennie managed to notice. Or were they intentionally watching her reactions for their matchmaking scheme?

She kept her suspicions to herself, pretending she didn't notice each time Luke's cherubs noticed. But she had much bigger goals in mind than courting someone from the other side of the country.

Scholars and the audience could readily rip apart her farming theory during her slot at the scientific congress tomorrow if she didn't have the new research incorporated. Research that hadn't been released during her last year at college. After her presentation, Clara McAdow promised the introduction to the Reverend Doctor Kelsey. Would he feel she'd earn her place at Oberlin? Without the repeated practices her friends encouraged, it wouldn't be possible at all. Bettina would continue not noticing the cherubic aunts noticing what she didn't want them to notice at all — her attraction to Luke.

She pinched the inside of a wrist to pull her mind back to the topic. "But can you imagine what this new knowledge means, Lydia?" Bettina leaned across the table in the center salon of the Montana pavilion grateful for the opportunity. What a blessing to rehearse and debate the ideas in her demonstration with the Lydia and Jennie, acting as devil's advocates. "Since the agriculturists here in Illinois discovered crop maturity advances as much as twelve miles per day from the south to the north, farming strategy could revolutionize how we produce food on a grander scale. Look at the hundreds of miles from south to north here alone."

Nodding, Jennie measured the distances. "What you're saying is we could gain approximately twenty-six more growing days across the country with this strategic crop planning and at least add a good portion of those growing days in Montana."

"Yes!" Bettina rejoiced.

Lydia waved a hand in the air. "Bettina, we have to take climate into account. Much of that south to north line is along mountainous terrain. If the chemistry isn't right—" she let the comment hang in the air like a hawk on a current. Sooner or later that hawk would dive for a mouse.

Bettina gave her a curious look. "The chemistry?"

Jennie and Lydia exchanged glances.

"It's like good relationships, if you sow on fertile ground and pull the weeds of misunder-standing regularly then your tender crop has a chance." Jennie added.

Bettina's brow crinkled. Were they talking about farming and harvests? "I'm sure you're right." She swept a hand from bottom to top over the map in the almanac. "By teaching farmers to plant crops with longer growth cycles farther south and plants with shorter growth cycles to the north..."

Out of the corner of her eye, she noticed Lydia and Jennie sent silent hand signals. As soon as she looked up, the ladies suddenly seemed to be smoothing a hairdo or skirt.

"Hmm? What were you saying, dear?" Lydia smiled. "Do go on."

Bettina finished her tactical theory, though another was forming having nothing to do with wheat or corn or feeding the masses. "...those extra days, amount to be determined by the clime and, uh, the chemistry can mean excess to send to cities. These tactics will raise farmer income while filling higher populace needs." She stood up fast as the two ladies snapped their eyes on the map with guilty looks. Cherubic, my foot! Their antics were far beyond simply noticing male-female attraction. These ladies may well be down right devious!

"I see. But you realize the last day of frost in Montana is not until quite late in May. Quite different than Illinois." Lydia pointed at the north area of the state.

Were they beleaguering the climate point for a reason? What logical or scientific point had she missed? Studying their uncharacteristically bland expressions, Bettina was sure the two had a secretive conversation going on they didn't want her to know about. But what?

"And this area might be up to a week earlier

some years, but not others depending on weather cycles. I think you're better suited to choosing crops for your comparison study by climes that would mature prior to the early known frost we can often experience. The length of growing days can be fickle, as can the heart."

Lydia nodded. "There's a natural harmony that has much to do with matching seed to soil type, water, humidity, sun, wind, pollination and so many other factors. Some of the chemistry you might be able to control. And then there's the synergy, the spark of creativity you cannot control, like love. That part of life is God's design."

"I have the distinct feeling you two are wanting this conversation to go in another direction or I've gone over the possible objections so many times I'm boring you."

"I certainly wouldn't have intruded," Lydia said in with a tongue-in-cheek tone, " would you, Jennie?"

"No, I'd never." She fluttered a fan as if offended. "But now that you've asked." Her expression turned motherly and compassion enveloped her every word.

"Yes, now that you've asked." Jennie nodded to Lydia. "Go ahead. He came to you for advice, didn't he then."

"We're concerned there's been a misunderstanding." Lydia watched closely as she asked, "What is it that keeps you avoiding our dear Luke?"

Mr. Edwards had talked to Lydia? Heat flushed up from Bettina's high collar as it had the first day they'd all met.

"Did he insult you?" She locked a hand onto a hip like a mother ready to set straight a son. "If an apology is in order then, by all means, give him the opportunity. After all, he's respected for his integrity."

"It's not about an apology. He hasn't done anything untoward." She leaned against the pavilion pillar leaving the large book open on the table. The sturdy support at her back helped with the two-against-one situation. "Mr. Edwards is, well, he is…" She wove her fingers together and focused into her palms. "Our beliefs in progress and the future are too different. We're too differ-ent." She let out her breath slowly at their disbe-lieving expressions. For ladies who loved to talk, their silence spoke in thunderous volumes. Her mother wouldn't let her get away with such a vague statement either. "You both know what I came for and it wasn't to find a man."

Then Jennie crossed her arms. "There's nothing saying you can't find both."

"It's not that he isn't a very attractive man, Jennie, he is. He's going to make some woman a very good husband. He's wildly handsome, confi-dent, caring, kind—"

"Just not for you even though you find him so appealing?"

Appealing. Apt description. "No, not for me. I don't want to be sidetracked from the dreams in my heart. His "dreams are very different from mine.""

She reached out a hand to her new friend. "You understand, don't you?" she asked as Jennie clasped both hands over Bettina's. Jennie's hands felt so gentle and compassion flowed from her making Bettina's words so much harder. "A mine owner. No, I just can't fathom the destruction. And how he could send other men into danger?" The comforting grasp encouraged her. "If there isn't a common goal then it's too dangerous. Why step into the fire?"

"Some pine trees need fire to propagate." Lydia smiled at Bettina's consternation. "Oh my dear, when you grow older you begin to realize that each person can have their own goal." Her knowing gaze held. "You don't have to chase the same dream to help the other reach theirs. Marriage is about helping your mate, not doing it for them."

"I hadn't thought of it that way." Bettina rubbed her teeth across her bottom lip. "But if those goals are complete opposites aren't the two destined to clash constantly?"

"You might think a little more on it." Jennie squeezed Bettina's hand once more. "I don't believe you've given him a fair chance. Do you?" She slid an arm around Bettina's shoulder in a gentle hug. "He's asked to speak with you and yet you turn him away. Learning more about what our Mr. Edwards does might help you see him in a different light. A hasty decision is the cause for many a mistake."

"We believe you've been a tad hasty. But then again, if it's not possible in your mind, I'm sure my niece wouldn't mind getting to know our Luke." She looked at Jennie with wide-eyed innocense. "Isn't that right?"

"Yes, yes. I'm sure there's potential with Janey." She wagged her head as if imparting solemn news. "You mustn't feel we're pushing the most eligible bachelor in Helena on you."

Lydia wobbled her head too. "No, no you mustn't. Although it occurs to me you've assumed the outcome without proper research. One must be sure of their facts." Another of her stunning steely-eyed gazes pinned Bettina like a moth on a board. "A scientist never assumes an outcome without testing her theories." She then drew a finger down a page of Bettina's book. "No, I don't think such a fine scientist as yourself would do such a thing."

Even with the older women's wisdom rolling through her mind, Bettina couldn't come up with any option that would offer compromise to a man who owned a mine, living off the sweat and blood of others. But feelings she didn't expect reared up at the thought of this Janey capturing his attention. Feelings she didn't like one bit. What did she want with a rich mine owner when her own father died in a coal mine poor as could be? But was it fair to

Luke Edwards, the way she'd locked him out with no explanation? A good scientist at least observes the facts. A lady, however, offered courtesy to those she disagreed with. But would mending that fence leave her heart open to—

"You sent for me, Mrs. Fitch?" Luke strode to the table, nearly out of breath. "What's the emergency?" He gave a curt dip of his head to Bettina, though his eyes lingered on hers.

Bettina's eyes widened as she stepped back. "Emergency?" She looked up into his blue eyes. "Oh, I feel terrible. I've been going on and on about the Illinois discovery. Forgive me, Lydia and Jennie. Please take care of whatever it is you must do. I'm happy to watch the display for you."

Lydia deepened into a pink one shade deeper than the bitterroot's petals. "Dear boy, there's no emergency." She glanced at Bettina. "I simply sent one of the ladies to ask that you stop in when you had a chance."

"When I—"

Now she understood how he must feel with all his matrimony prospects being managed by such helpful friends. They'd kept her talking long enough for another to fetch him. Was the mention of Janey's interest another ruse then, too.

"Would you be a dear and explain to Miss Gilbert here what your plans are for your mines? A little on how you've changed practices to protect nature will do. Of course we all know the strides you've made in mining safety protocol."

Bettina would have turned tail and skedaddled out of there. But Lydia put an arm around her waist and wasn't letting go.

He looked between the two women. His eyes narrowed. "I think I'm on to you, Mrs. Fitch."

"Me? I have no idea what you could mean, dear boy." She feigned the same innocent, wide-eyed expression Bettina had experienced only moments before. "Go ahead, I'm sure this is going to fasci-nate us."

"If Miss Gilbert is at all interested, she's welcome to attend one of my talks at the Mines and Mining Building. I'll be sure to go into detail for her." He gave them all a nod. "Enjoy your after-noon, ladies."

"Oh, my dear," Mrs. Fitch's face looked worried as she watched him walk out. "You must at least go to one of his talks. It appears that though he may not have offended you, you certainly did offend him."

CHAPTER 6

Luke had been by the Woman's Building a few times in the last few weeks. He'd managed to find reasons check in with the ladies, but only garnered a good snubbing from Bettina Gilbert for his trouble. For a man who ran several mining crews of rough characters, that woman could make his knees quake with a single glance. Something no other had done.

The ladies made sure to continue their quest to find his perfect mate while Mrs. Fitch made a few attempts to smooth the way for him with Bettina. But nothing swayed her. He'd met more women in those few weeks and he couldn't remember half of them. Then why couldn't he forget her?

He knew when he spotted Mrs. Fitch listening politely to his presentation about silver, gold, copper, and other Montana mining successes she had news of some sort—or she'd given up on patching his rift with Bettina.

"Though mining can be competitive, the Kimberley Diamond Mining Company has under-written this entire exhibit with contributions from more than twelve counties sharing over fifty tons of specimens. The gold nuggets you see are dwarfed by the forty-eight ounce giant here." He placed a hand on the mother of gold nuggets, enjoying the amazement of his guests. "In addition, please note the sapphires, rubies, and garnets native to our mountainous state."

He moved to steps near the middle of the room. "Now I'd like to share a little about our Lady Justice. Joined together with mining companies across the state to promote the health of the indus-try, the solid gold plinth she stands on is on loan from the Spotted Horse Mine of Maiden, Montana. It measures two feet on each side. The lady herself is solid silver belonging to two men loaning equal measures for the mold pouring. She holds a level balancing equal measures of silver and gold. Her sword denotes the battle of justice for all."

The mingling nations were often represented in the fair-goers through exotic dress, language, and customs. He knew some followed his gestures, but couldn't follow all of his words. "You'll note our twelve-foot tall Lady Justice has her eyes uncov-ered." He pointed up. Then for the sake of the foreign children, Luke bent his knees and flashed his fingers open in front of his eyes garnering a round of giggles.

"In researching the concept of justice portrayed this way through the centuries, we discovered she's only been blindfolded the last two hundred years. Though often portrayed in marble and stone, she'd never been immortalized in a precious material like silver. In Montana, we don't want Lady Justice to turn a blind eye so there is no blindfold. Contrary to the idea that she be blind to individuals, we believe in individual freedom in Montana. Are there any questions?"

Mrs. Fitch raised her hand.

He took a breath drawing deep. "Yes, ma'am."

"My niece would like to know who modeled for the lovely statue?"

She wouldn't have asked that particular question normally. He knew exactly how she felt about the choice of model. Now he knew Mrs. Fitch's purpose in attending another one of his talks— she'd resumed her matchmaking. So, she'd made no progress with Bettina either.

After the disaster with Bettina, her avoidance communicated volumes. She wasn't interested. His heart squeezed. It was hopeless. Was it time to give up and turn himself over to the three women who had his wellbeing at heart? If he wanted a wife, then he had to get that pretty botanist out of his head.

Her niece stepped into view. Jeanne. No.

Joanne. No. J, it starts with a J. With any luck one of them would drop the lovely girl's name before he had to admit not remembering it. He smiled at the young lady and warmed as she returned a smile.

"That's a wonderful question, Mrs. Fitch." He waggled a finger with a little dramatic flair bringing grins from the little ones dressed in colorful satins. "And a controversial one as well. Montanans had their own idea of a feminine model who was chosen from young ladies who lived in our state. But our executive director over the Montana World's Fair Board, Mr. Bickford, and the artist had other ideas. Ada Rehan, the famous New York actress, stands before you immortalized in precious metal."

The crowd oohed at the mention of the well-known actress, with a bit of a questionable reputation, and the story-behind-the-scenes that Luke shared.

"Our citizenry didn't appreciate that a non-resident actress should be chosen over the epitome of Montana womanhood. However, Miss Rehan fit sixty-two of the sixty-eight artistic points of beauty. Who can argue with an artist and win?" He chuckled with the attendees that understood English. "Our newspapers still tried to mount a campaign up to the last moment. We are a stubborn people." He lifted his arms then let his hands fall against his legs. Another short burst of appreciation for his light wit rippled around the central space inside the Grecian columns surrounding the booth.

"Miss Rehan posed for the statue mold. Then the mold was poured from Montana silver provided through the First National Bank of Helena due to the work of Mr. Samuel T. Hauser and Mr. William A. Clark of Butte on March 18th."

Janey sidled closer to her aunt and sent him a flirty smile. Janey, that's it! Perhaps he should open his mind if Mrs. Fitch believed she could be a good wife. She was of age and very attractive. Could she relax and converse as they grew to know one another? He could at least try. How could one form an opinion in such a short first visit? Then again, he'd only had an afternoon visit with—

"Mr. Edwards?"

He knew that voice and his blood raced at the sound of it. "Yes, another question." He searched the growing crowd for the presence of the woman he'd hoped might give him a chance.

People filled in the standing room only aisles inside and around the mining exhibit. Touted as a not-to-be-missed feature, the Montana mining and minerals hadn't let up in its popularity in the first month.

"Mr. Edwards, do tell us if you think you might run out of this precious silver any time soon?"

"Excellent question, Miss Gilbert." Was that it? Had she worried about his livelihood since the silver pricing downturn began? She didn't seem like the type to be that concerned about security, but what did he know of a woman's mind? He could quell that concern. "As a matter of fact, no. The silver deposits in Montana are nowhere near running out regardless of the silver act redirecting purchases to the gold standard. Last year alone our state produced enough silver to cast a thousand of these statues and had plenty to have minted a thousand silver dollars."

The crowd gasped at the statement.

"You mean that ripping the land apart for financial gain is worth the scars left behind? What about future generations? What about rehabilitating the natural resources? What about the danger to the men?" She had a fierce expression. "What a waste of God's green earth." She turned to leave.

"Kindly let me offer a response, Miss Gilbert."

"I can't imagine that you'd have one, Mr. Edwards."

"But I do." The crowd parted as he stepped down off the dais at Lady Justice's feet and walked into the hall.

Many onlookers followed him while others merely needed to turn a bit.

"Tell me about how cities are built without wood or quarries. How should dentists fill cavities without gold? And without coal, how can the iron horse ship food to distant places or warm tenements?"

"I'm sure those things—"

"Are important to civilization?"

A smattering of applause accompanied his debate.

"Of course." Her back stiffened. "However, we must act with conservation and safety in mind. When the land is changed and it can't regenerate then what direction have we set but one for destruction?"

Now Bettina's words were met with applause. She nodded appreciation at the affirmation. They'd effectively created a public debate, and those gathered embraced it as an oratory event.

"And copper, Miss Gilbert? Copper conducts electricity." There must be copper in his veins because she'd managed to get his blood spiking and surging. "How do you suppose we provide electricity to cities, hospitals, or homes in the future if we have no mining for this resource?"

"Resources that may not be replenished if done irresponsibly."

Another pat, pat, patter of audience appreciation.

"You are assuming all mining is done irresponsibly, Miss Gilbert, civilization demands support. Through our mining and mineral opportunities we better the lives of everyone on this planet." Isn't that what she'd told him she wanted? To uplift the lives of the less fortunate?

"What about the lives of those men in the mines? Tell me your answer to that, Mr. Edwards." She crossed her arms and tapped a foot.

"You tell 'im, Miss!" A voice called out.

"I'll tell you about the jobs that responsible mining provides, and then I'll tell you about all the families those working men feed. Without mining, our entire nation would lose a major industry for our populace. Children would go hungry with fathers out of work. Do you propose we let that happen?"

"He's got a point." Another said. "A job's a job when we got little ones to feed."

Mrs. Fitch moved into his line of sight. She gave three sharp shakes of her head.

If he didn't end this impromptu debate, there might be no coming back with Bettina Gilbert—and they needed to talk. She had to give him the chance to clear up the misunderstanding that he couldn't comprehend. "Ladies and gentlemen, thank you for attending. Be sure to see my two favorites, the Statue of Liberty made of salt and visit the Silver Lady next door in the Colorado pavilion on your tour through the building. Thank you."

The crowd applauded. A few voiced their appreciation while a family from somewhere in Asia ducked their heads to him in a small bow.

Bettina whirled and stomped away.

Was it mining, safety, or something else that bothered her? Luke glanced around for Mrs. Fitch and Janey.

Mrs. Fitch threaded through a few people. Was she disappointed or delighted Bettina offered less competition to her niece? "Oh, Luke. Dear boy, how could you?"

Disappointed. He turned his palms up and sighed. "What was I supposed to do? She wants to help people, but doesn't understand there's more to it than feeding them bread." Then he pushed his hands into his pockets and stared at his shoes.

"She's a smart girl. She will understand if you take the time to help her."

"She doesn't want to have anything to do with me anyway." He looked down the aisle she'd exited. A city girl who despises his way of life would be the worst choice for a miner's wife, wouldn't she? So why couldn't he get her out of his head? Why did his heart feel as heavy as the statue he'd just talked about?

"I think you're misreading the situation." She patted his arm. "If she didn't want to know you then she wouldn't have come. She's been miserable though trying not to let anyone notice. Time to stop avoiding the conflict and go get started on securing yourself a wife."

"Aunt Lydia? Mr. Edwards?" Janey managed to squeeze through the crowd and join the two of them. She looked fetching in a light pink day dress and straw sunhat covered in an array of pink and white flowers. The pink bow at the right of her chin brought a youthful color to her complexion. "Is everything all right?"

"All will be fine. Won't it, Luke?"

Why couldn't he have fallen for a sweet, simple girl like Janey? "It's just Luke to my friends." He took her fingers in a genteel greeting. "Janey, thank you for coming. Did you enjoy the presentation?" He asked as he released her hand.

"It was a bit technical for me, but I enjoyed your beautiful speaking voice."

"Ah. Technical. That could dampen my tour for some." He looked at Mrs. Fitch to add her opinion.

She merely glanced away at the stack of copper bricks behind Lady Justice.

"I'll take that under advisement."

Janey fluttered her lashes seeming to preen that he'd considered her thoughts a valuable commentary.

Mrs. Fitch glanced between Janey and Luke, gave an almost imperceptible tilt of her head the direction Bettina had gone and pressed her lips together. Then she raised her brows, signaling with her eyes down the aisle, as if to say, "*I think you have somewhere to be young man.*"

If she offered, albeit silently, he'd take her advice and go. "Pleased to see you again, Janey. Will you ladies excuse me?"

He waved to one of the other men in the far corner to take over and heard Mrs. Fitch behind him.

"He is a bit too slow for you, Janey, dear. I have another fellow much more charming in mind."

Luke choked back a laugh as he headed out the south entrance, grand doors that led to the lagoon in the center of the Court of Honor.

"Bettina!" He couldn't believe it. She stood in front of the colossal Columbus fountain depicting his arrival in America. She turned at his call with red-rimmed eyes and tears streaking down her cheeks that could create a fountain of their own.

Shame for the way he'd spoken to her in public doused any fire he'd felt at her words. Somehow they had to clear up the mess they'd made—and it started with humbling himself for her. He stood beside her waiting for her to accept his presence.

She turned back to the water, trickling off the fountain's oars and splashing below Columbus' feet as he stood on the bow searching for the shore. Could they find dry ground together?

"Bettina, will you forgive me?" He said it softly without demand or expectation that she should.

She looked up into his eyes, searched his soul for what seemed an eternity, and then offered her own apology. "I've made assumptions about you and judged you harshly without merit. The apology is mine to give, not yours. By meeting you, I came face-to-face for the first time with the kind of monster I blamed for my father's death in a mine collapse." She dropped her eyes to his chest. "I'm an orphan."

"But you speak of your parents as if they're alive."

"I'm adopted. Adopted by the doctor that...the doctor that couldn't save my mother. But he could save me, as sick as I was with typhoid, too."

"I don't know what to say."

"Just listen. When I heard you were rich, that made me angrier that you made money off of the suffering of others. The monster in my mind I'd built up all these years finally had a face."

"But—"

"I know." She turned to face Columbus again as if she drew strength from the cascade of water helping her pour out her story. "You aren't a monster. The more I've watched you, the more I've discovered a man of kindness and integrity. A man who cared about others and served without resentment. You brought water, food, and," she let out an ironic chuckle, "you made sure everyone else was taken care of first, before yourself. I couldn't understand it or release that monstrous picture I'd built in my head even though my eyes could see."

He lifted a hand, palm up, and held his breath. Would she touch him?

She placed hers in his and a jolt rocketed through his body. They watched the light reflect on the splashing surface. The mist cooled the hot summer air around them. He released that breath slowly, evenly so as not to disturb the moment and listened to her heart.

"After my father's death, my mother had no choice but to move us into the city." She jutted her chin motioning toward the town. "Chicago. She did everything she could to survive. Things she shouldn't have had to if my father hadn't died. Then typhoid struck and people started dying in the epidemic. First my little brother, he was four." She swiped away a tear dangling from her chin. "Then my mother fell ill for weeks and still tried to take in laundry. Eventually she caught pneumonia. That finally took her. She hadn't worked in so long we had no food. I begged on the streets while she slept, tried to help wash clothes, and began to get ill as well. But a neighbor took pity and called for a doctor to look in on our family."

He tightened his hold on her hand wishing he could carry this pain for her. Pain he'd had no idea he churned up like tailings from a mine poisoning the very ground it'd come from. That she could bear up under the weight of it made him admire her that much more for her strength. For the desire to change the circumstances for others like her.

"On my mother's deathbed, she told me not to be afraid, that the doctor was here to help me. He wouldn't leave me alone." She smiled at the ground and then gave him a sidelong glance that said she understood as an adult now what her mother had tried to do for her. "I don't know whether he felt pressured or some form of guilt, but that doctor agreed to take care of me. He promised my mother he wouldn't leave me behind when she breathed her last."

Her mouth worked a moment, though no words came out. She took a deep breath. "Right there, in that hovel, she gave me into the safe keeping of the doctor. And then she was gone." She whispered the words as if reliving the moment. "I was eight. He kept that promise even refusing the neighbor's payment. He knew he was a very poor man." She smiled, her tears drying. "He still says he got the better part of the deal in a daughter. My parents adopted me, educated me, and have never treated me with anything but the deepest of love. I'm so blessed. But there are so many others that have no one to rescue them from starvation, disease, and poverty. That's why I'm so driven. Someone has to help the others."

She inspired him to want to do more, to help her live out the calling on her that seemed God ordained. If only he'd known sooner. "I'm so sorry my ignorance caused you any further pain."

She shook her head, the tiny ribbons down her back fluttered as the breeze off the water picked them up and dropped them back down. "You've done nothing wrong. What I want to say is thank you. Thank you for helping me face my childhood demons and forgive people caught in circumstances beyond their control." She blinked in the sunshine as she gazed up at him. "If you consider me unworthy of your—"

Luke took her in his arms and held her close. "I consider you most precious." Then he realized the liberty he taken and released her. But he whispered into her ear as he pressed her hand to his heart, "The most precious of women."

CHAPTER 7

JULY 7, 1893

BETTINA'S KNEES TREMBLED FASTER THAN
a lady's fan flickered on a blistering day. She knew
her talk was well received. She'd answered every
discussion question from the audience with
aplomb, according to her father. He'd said it with
his chest puffed out while Mama beamed on his
arm. Yet her heart rat-a-tatted like the drummer in
the John Phillips Souza concert Luke had taken her
to last week. Had she impressed Reverend Doctor
Kelsey enough to win the position at Oberlin?

First he shook hands with her father, congratu-
lating him on raising a fine young scientist. Then
he turned to her mother and praised her skills of

turning out such a gracious child. Then, finally, he addressed Bettina.

"Young lady, you have a quick mind and very thorough research methods. You've worked hard to create a possible plan to help the masses."

She brightened. He saw her vision, her—

"But I see a flaw in your theory."

Her stomach hit her boots and the blood in her body followed it. "A flaw?"

"You focus too much on the overview to bring about results because of the intensity of your passion to save the poor right now. Would you consider coming at your research from a more practical angle?"

Practical? Wasn't that the entire basis of her theory? That it could be put to use for practical solutions? "Please, sir, where might I improve?"

His face relaxed into an inviting smile. "That's exactly the question I wanted to hear. It shows me you're open to criticism that will help you grow as a scientist and as you undertake this project long-term."

"But the flaw?"

"Your vision will give you the passion to keep working toward your goal. However…"

Flaw. However. She hung on his words, leaning in to understand.

"…I'd advise you to focus not en masse, but the on the exponential. Study the cause at its root or we cannot repeat the result intentionally. Do you look over a field of wheat and say it grows because of the sun?" He pulled the boutonnière from his lapel. "If I dissect this flower and glean all I can from it, but I haven't grown it and observed it in various situations how can I say what I observed will be repeatable?" He replaced the button mum. "By starting with one I can determine how and why it thrives best. Then, once I understand how the flower flourishes I can expand to help it and others like it prosper. Understand the organism at its most elemental level and you'll be able to build outward from there. Would you consider it wise to include observations from others? Consult with those who work the crops. What have they observed year after year? You have much work to do yet."

His wisdom opened her eyes to the flaw. She didn't have enough information to guarantee success yet. "Yes, I understand. Thank you, sir."

"I came because your application stood out. Rarely do I see such high marks in laboratory work. With your parents approval, I'm extending an invitation to be part of my team. I see in you one who desires to make the world a better place through your science—"

She opened her mouth to respond, but he held up a hand.

"— if you'll temper your enthusiasm for imme-diacy and focus on causal research. Can you cap that passion and channel it into tedious work for the greater good?"

She''d never felt such elation before. "Yes, yes sir!"

"Good. Then we'll see you this fall at Oberlin."

She stared after the good doctor. He hadn't even asked for a reference letter!

CHAPTER 8

"My darling girl, we couldn't be more proud.
But it's for men to be so driven. Shouldn't your
education be enough?" Mama wanted grandchil-
dren, specifically granddaughters. One surprise
daughter hadn't been enough with four boisterous
sons.

She hadn't been part of Bettina's early childhood to dress her and show her off as a baby. But
Mama had a huge trousseau planned in a design
book collected page-by-page since she'd gained a
little girl. Especially since two sons, Robert, Jr. and
Daniel, produced a passel of boys, but not yet one
girl. Of course, neither Bruce nor George would
marry for another few years. "With what you know,
your children will be well educated. Goodness,
you'll rule any garden club in the city. Change is
made in the parlor, influencing people, not out in

the fields. Imagine the lives you could influence." Marion Gilbert swept her hands out as if gathering the grand downtown Chicago coffee house, where they sat, into her fold. Mama had a gift for gathering people to her and, once there, never letting them go. Her loyalty was renowned amongst those who knew her.

"Mama, botanists might belong to garden clubs but they don't plant pretty flowers for the hobby of it." She covered her mother's hand on the table. "Don't you understand I want to feed thousands of children through my science, not a few from my stove?"

Her mother slid back in her seat as if she'd been slapped. Tears glistened though she blinked rapidly. "I suppose being a mother isn't enough to contribute to society. I understand."

How had her passions insulted her mother so deeply? "Mama, that's not what I meant. Motherhood is truly God-inspired. But I'm not ready for that yet."

"You're twenty-two. How long do you think you have to pass on those brilliant genetics when you haven't even married yet?"

"I think what your mother means is—"

"Robert, I know what I mean." The tears gone, red spots on her cheeks flashed the signal a storm would let loose any second. Bettina's adventure gene seemed a wild card to Mama. Inexplicable.

"What if I could influence farmers with my

discoveries? What if each person I educate could affect the lives of hundreds or thousands? Can't you see how that would make daily life better for all mothers?" She bowed her head. "What if what I achieve could have helped a mother," Bettina's voice thickened, "who died like mine? Couldn't that be enough?"

Ever the peacemaker, Papa brushed the subject aside. "Bettina, we understand how important it is to you to be involved in bettering society. We've never besmirched your beginnings, nor would we now. Your birth parents were hard working, honorable people. It's only natural you want to help those who weren't as fortunate. Accept the position, if you wish—" he held up a hand to stay Mama's objection. Then he looked at her as he finished, "…at least it brings you home to Cleveland. We'll talk more about other future prospects then."

"There are plenty of important volunteer opportunities for married women right in Cleveland."

Papa closed his eyes for a moment.

"Mama—"

"Bettina." Her father's eyes opened and focused on her. His raised eyebrows and stern tone stopped any further discussion. He snapped for the waiter. "The end of the summer, then we'll talk in the privacy of our home where discussions such as this belong."

CHAPTER 9

THE SIX-BLOCK WALK wouldn't have been too difficult, but the July's temperatures already rose steadily into the nineties by mid-morning on clear days. With not much of a breeze off the lake, she'd be a puddle of perspiration before starting her shift to break the ladies for luncheon. With the heat, and Mama's worry for her safety in the city, ensconced in safe transportation rather than alone on the streets might appease her overly protective sensibilities.

Right now Bettina did not need to challenge her mother further. She would keep using public transportation as she'd agreed when they rented the city townhouse for the summer.

Bettina boarded the World's Fair omnibus leaving her parents to a little Friday shopping. She chose the first empty seat toward the back door hoping for a little draft of fresh air, and drew out her hand fan. Flicking her wrist, fanning away the scent of horse and human, the morning celebratory brunch with her parents took longer than she expected. But then again, they seemed bent on convincing her against going anywhere away from home.

How could she help the children of Chicago or any other city if she never experienced the farms or understood the challenges of farmers outside the sprawl of buildings? Traveling the nearby countryside couldn't be that outrageous as part of her position at Oberlin. Why couldn't she have waited to share the details of the position until the summer ended?

Bettina waved out the side window to her parents as the carriage moved away from the curb. "I'll be home before dark or I'll send word and be sure I have an escort." She called a reassurance to Mama who waved back until she was out of sight. Knowing Mama, the discussion with Papa had just begun. Bettina leaned her head against the wooden wall. She was already spent from the intense emotions of the day, and it was only nine a.m.

The horses clipped along at a brisk pace toward the city-side entrance. A few blocks shy of their goal one of the horses whinnied. The carriage lurched sliding Bettina a few inches on her bench into the woman next to her.

Another loud neighing at the sound of a crack

and the carriage whipped forward as the nose crashed into the street. Bettina let out a screech with the yells and screams of other passengers adding to the chaos and then smacked headlong into the bench in front of her.

As the horses high-pitched whinnies continued the omnibus carriage wrenched forward ripping. The back door flew wide as her body slammed into it then she tumbled over the steps just missing the edges as they burst up toward her with the runaway draft team's frantic thrust forward.

She thudded to the street and rolled in a tangle of skirts, arms and legs flailing, as the brightly painted vehicle careened onto a corner and then flopped onto its side as the horses dragged it another twenty feet.

As Bettina painfully pushed herself up to see the damage, a crowd ran to help her.

CHAPTER 10

"WHERE HAS SHE GONE?" He'd wanted to congratulate her on a speech well done. To tell her Montana needed scientists like her. To tell her he needed her.

"I believe her parents took her to a restaurant just outside the grounds to celebrate." Mrs. Fitch rattled off. "I don't think she could eat a bite beforehand. For an early morning event, that was a large audience. Can you imagine a young thing like that speaking to fifteen hundred people? Brilliant girl, just brilliant!"

Disappointment permeated Luke like a cold, dark mine's damp air when the vein petered out.

Mrs. Fitch gave Luke a sympathetic look. "They'd never have found seating inside at breakfast time, you know. Those lines don't seem to go down no matter what time of day or night."

Luke paced the pavilion floor in the Woman's Building. One thing Bettina was not—late. She had some sort of internal clockwork in her head he couldn't explain. Worry gnawed in his gut the way mice worked a rope. He'd slipped away from the auditorium this morning so as not to disturb her discussion with the Reverend Doctor Kelsey. Though he prayed for her as he left the building, he also prayed for God's will. Luke hoped God's will aligned more with his desire to marry Bettina than Bettina's desire to work for the scientist. Would she give up her dream to love him?

But he knew better than to superimpose his will above God's. It didn't hurt to let the Almighty know what he wanted though. And she'd planned to meet him at the booth. She'd said as much.

"I'm sure she was simply detained discussing her speechifying success with her parents." Mrs. Fitch soothed. "She was quite dazzling."

"Yes, she was." Quite, he brooded. "But I need to see her before I go. She doesn't know."

"You haven't told her yet?"

"No, I didn't want to cause her any stress before her presentation at the congress. She was as nervous as a puppy around fireworks this last week."

"Mm." Mrs. Fitch hummed an agreement as she rearranged the seating, putting chairs back into the inviting arc she preferred. "When do you leave?"

He picked up a chair and walked it over as she

pointed out the spot to leave it. "In the morning. There just isn't any choice left to me."

"No, I suppose there isn't." She put a hand on his arm. Mrs. Fitch's eyes told the story of years. Years of watching men build the frontier by scratching in the ground to create civilization. "I've learned in my time that things have a way of coming around for the better."

"I hope you're right, Mrs. Fitch. I hope you're right."

"Luke, don't leave things hanging if you want one special bride." She patted his arm. "Go find her and spend the day together before you get on the train." She dug in her satchel. "I have Bettina's schedule. You know she loves her schedule. No surprises for that girl. I'm sure as snow falls in the mountains that she's written which restaurant she'd be at with her parents if her talk went well."

She held a paper close to her nose. "Yes, here it is." Handing it over, she suggested, "Pray about it. Let her know how you feel. Then let God direct her path." She tipped her head and shrugged. "Maybe she'll even go with you. But you won't know unless you take the chance. And you, my boy, have nothing to lose."

"Thank you, Mrs. Fitch."

"Off with you now." She flicked her fingers at him. "Go get your girl."

～

LUKE GRABBED FOR THE THICK LEATHER harness. He bellowed over the city noise in a deep baritone, "Whoa, whoa there."

As the draft horse drew to a dancing stop, he gentled his voice to calm the team fighting the adrenaline it'd taken to capture them and their runaway omnibus.

Passersby raced to help him rescue and then comfort the injured passengers. He lifted several women out of the sideways vehicle through the broken windows. He checked inside for any more unable to get out on their own and found it empty, jumbled with belongings.

Then he spotted Bettina's favorite purple ostrich plumed hat laying in the street! He snatched it up. She was here somewhere. Then he noticed a shawl being draped over one of the women. Oh, God, let her be alive.

"Bettina Gilbert!" He yelled through cupped hands down the city street the direction the horses had come. A splintered wheel, spokes poking up, lay in the center of the road. He sidestepped it racing toward another circle of people as a man redirected other carriages to turn and go around the block before reaching 61st Street.

As he jogged closer, he glimpsed a dove gray skirt like Bettina's. "Please, let me through. Let me through." He caught a glimpse of her bruised face. He gently pressed people aside. "Please, excuse me. Let me through. I'm her friend."

She lay on the ground, rumpled and dirtied, but surprisingly in better condition than he'd expected. Hunkering down, he asked, "How badly hurt are you?"

She touched her elbow where a little tear showed a scrape. "A few bumps, but if you'll help me up—"

Shuffling his arms under her knees and shoulders, Luke clasped her to him. "I was terrified."

She gave a breathy laugh. "Me, too." Her fingers touched the bruise on her forehead.

Luke stood and the gathered crowd let him through with a few pats on his shoulders as he carried Bettina to the sidewalk. He set her down on the curb and held her at arm's length as he looked her up and down. "Are you sure you're not badly injured?"

She looked up into his eyes making him want to melt with relief. "I have a few bumps and a nice, tidy headache. But the worst was I had the wind knocked out of me." She sought to look past him. "Is anyone else hurt?" She winced and pressed a palm against her forehead.

"A few more than others. But they're being taken care of now." He wouldn't worry her further. The news would come soon enough how close she came to the gates of Heaven.

"That's good." She leaned against his shoulder. "I think I should change clothes before going back to the booth."

"Mrs. Fitch gave you the rest of the day off. I was coming to ask you to spend it with me. But it might be best to take you home to rest. Your father needs to examine you."

She sat up straight. "No! I'd prefer we keep this incident between us. If Mama caught wind that I'd been…oh no, no, no." She pushed against his body. "I'll go home, but only to freshen up and change."

"All right." He looked her over one more time. She really did seem fine, by God's grace. "But your mother couldn't help seeing that goose egg."

"I have a lovely sun hat that will do the trick for now."

He remembered the plumed hat and held it out to her. They both laughed at the sorry state of the fancy hair piece. The plumes crooked at odd angles and the cap's colors turned a muddle of brown and purple from the street refuse.

"I think this one has seen its day." She lifted a plume and it broke in two. "Shall we go?"

"Then, if you're up to it, I'd like to take you somewhere peaceful where we can have a quiet conversation while you rest a bit. No rickshaw today rattling that lovely head of yours."

"I'm sure I'll be up to it." A starry smile spread across her lips. Lips he wanted to taste more than candied caramel corn or sparkling sodas or the world's most enticing delicacy. Tonight he would.

CHAPTER 11

"Bettina, what I'm trying to say is I have to go home to Montana. Tomorrow morning. My train leaves at seven." The same time she'd presented today. Could he see seven in the morning the same again?

"Why now? There's still months left of the exposition."

He sat with her on the island park bench. The craze of the carriage crash, crowds, and commotion of the fair across the canal. Surrounded by the peace of the Japanese lanterns glowing along the shaded path and the respite of the Wooded Island, Luke took her hand in his. "Would you come with me?"

"Why can't you stay?"

"It's the silver. Since the government has

replaced it with the gold standard, silver has been falling. Falling hard enough that I have to close one of my mines. Now the Reading Railroad has entered bankruptcy, steel has fallen. It's a deluge of one thing after another. I have no choice but to close one of my mines and let men go." His eyes blinked hard several times.

"Will you come back?"

"I don't know," his voice failed. "I don't know when or if I'll be able to come back." His shoulders slumped a tad.

She watched the way his thumb moved over her knuckles in soft brushes and her heart broke for him. "What happens now?"

"I'll try to relocate as many men as I can from the silver mine to the copper. With electricity coming on strong across the country, it's possible the demand will remain. But there aren't enough jobs in one mine to absorb all the men from another." Luke ran a hand across the back of his neck. "I'm putting dozens and dozens of men out of work. Men who have families to feed."

His pain flooded her body. She finally understood the other side of the mining equation. The sense of responsibility he felt for people who relied on his jobs to survive. "I'm so sorry."

"To look a man in the eye, while you know his fate yet he does not?" His face reddened while he rasped out, "That burden should belong to God only."

She wanted to hold him. To tell him she loved him and would stand by him through this terrible time. And yet, as she ached for Luke and the painful decisions he must make that would affect so many lives, so many families, Bettina knew the heaviness of that burden well. Knew the burden of looking a man in the eye and telling him what would change his fate. She knew she had to tell Luke no.

She lifted her gaze to his, tears burning, and swayed into his arms like the cobra who'd danced to the flute over at the International displays. A cobra whose grace belied the bite to come. He lowered his mouth to hers. A kiss she wanted to lock in her heart forever. Her first kiss—and her last. There'd be no other for her. She knew that as much as she knew he'd come for a wife. Salty tears mingled at their lips. She dropped her arms from his warm, strong neck.

He lifted his head and searched her wet face. "You're not coming then, are you?"

Bettina scrubbed a hand across her cheeks and looked away at the same green grass that she'd told Luke breathed life into the world. The same green grass she'd study to find out why it grew so fast almost anywhere while other plants didn't. Green grass that tickled her nostrils with the scent of heaven after a rain. She kept her eyes glued on the green grass and gave an almost imperceptive, shake of her head. "How can I?"

"You can because you love me."

"And I love my family." She raised her face to his then. "You don't understand." She stood and took a step backward.

"No." Luke stood and reached out for her, but Bettina backed away again. "I don't."

"My parents never considered turning me out or giving me over to an institution. Instead, they made me part of the family. My education, it's all because they poured love into me. I need to use these gifts, Luke. I have to honor all they've done for me."

"If they love you, they want you to be happy."

"But don't you see? I can't be happy if I bring them even a second of pain. All I am I owe to people who owed me nothing and yet gave me everything." She leaned toward Luke, toward the life she wanted but couldn't have. "I cannot now or ever hand them betrayal like that. Could you?" She waited for him to respond. "If you could, I just couldn't—"

He gathered her against him, tangled his fingers into her hair, and held her tight. "I love you."

"Luke, I do love you. But since I can't go with you, I—" Bettina swallowed back the lump in her throat that seemed to grow thorns, jabbing sharply as blood pounded hard in her head. "I think you should take Janey with you." Tears coursed down her face, wetting his shirtfront. "I need to know you'll be happy then I'll be happy, too, every time I think of you." Every day. She disentangled herself and walked into the life she'd chosen.

EPILOGUE

NOVEMBER 1, 1893

Helena, Montana

LUKE MET FRANKIE SHANAHAN ON THE porch as he tied his horse off. "Haven't seen you in a while. Did you bring me some mail?"

The teenager who once led a group of newsies now held a more trusted messenger position when not in school. "Got a letter from someone named Miss Gilbert?"

Luke bounded down the steps into his yard. "Let's see it."

Frankie flipped open his saddle pack and pulled out a newspaper and a tan envelope.

Luke scanned the message and looked at Frankie in awe. "She's coming." He hooted, tossing his hat in the air and grabbing the sixteen-year old in a bear hug. "She's coming now!"

Both men, one nearly to adulthood and one on the cusp of matrimony, dusted off their hats grinning like fools. "She'll be on the same train as our contingent returning from the exposition!"

"I'm right pleased for you Mr. Edwards."

Today! "The train's due in a couple hours."

"I wouldn't be too far behind it then. Some other fella might be snatchin' yer girl." So matter of fact.

Luke laughed. Frankie laughed. But they both knew the truth of his words.

He sobered. Then churned up dust as he took off toward the barn. "Frankie, there'll be an extra tip in your pay this month." He hollered over his shoulder. "You've made me a happy man!"

A few hours later, Luke checked each window as the train pulled into the station. He ran along the length of it searching as passengers stepped off thrilled to be home.

Then time froze as Bettina stopped in the doorway searching the platform until she found him. Her smile bloomed beckoning him to her as if a golden lasso dropped around his heart and tugged.

Bettina held out a hand, clad in the fine Spanish lace gloves he'd given her that first day, and took his, walking straight into his arms. Arms that had ached to hold her against a heart that had shredded in Chicago. He breathed in her scent as he pressed his mouth against her neck. "You came."

He brushed off a tap on his shoulder.

A deep throat cleared right next to him. "Excuse me, son, but that's my daughter and you haven't asked my permission to be so free with her."

Luke jumped back and stuttered. "Your—your—" He shot a look from the taller, well-dressed man in a vested suit to Bettina and back again. He turned to Bettina, one thought on his mind. "You did come to marry me, right?"

"Yes." Bettina's musical laugh soothed his sore soul. "Mr. Luke Edwards I'd like to introduce my father, Mr. Robert Gilbert, and my mother, Mrs. Marion Gilbert."

He greeted them, but noticed several men hanging around the train watching with curious interest. He wasn't taking any chances with the most precious woman in the world. "Sir, if you'd give me permission to marry your daughter I promise to love and protect her every day of my life."

"Wait a moment. I haven't finished." A mischievous smile played around her lips. "I'm sure you'd like to meet my brothers, their wives, and my nephews..."

As she named them all right down to her passle of nephews.

He took in the large family gathering around them under the awning of the small Helena train depot. He swallowed. She told him she'd never leave her family behind. How many were there? Shock must have registered on his face as he kept nodding at each person. "Uh, pleased to meet you. And you. And you…"

Mr. Gilbert held out his hand. "We're glad to meet you too, son."

Luke took it.

"Our little Bettina about pined away missing you. If I were to deny you I don't think she'd ever forgive me."

It took a moment to sink in, but then he grinned at his future father-in-law. "I'll do my best to see she's happy."

"Now let's see about making this official once we find our lodgings."

Nodding, he stared around the uneven circle. The sheer volume of them and the luggage being unloaded around them. What would he do with them all?

Bettina leaned in and whispered. "Papa has taken a position at St. John's Hospital as has my oldest brother. They're sending carriages around." She pointed to another man corralling a toddler. "You remember that's Daniel."

No, but he nodded.

"Daniel will be working as a pharmacist. He has yet to determine whether the local pharmacy has room or if he'll need to open another."

"Ah. I see." He gazed at her as she spoke. "And what about you and your dreams? You're giving them up for me?"

Her brows drew together. "Absolutely not." She folded her arms and announced, "I've been given a grant to study farming techniques in the west as part of a greater program being run through Oberlin."

He moved to wrap his arms around her and then stopped, remembering Mr. Gilbert's warning. "May I?"

"You may."

He kissed his bride soundly as he heard Mrs. Fitch say, "There, you see, we've brought home seven medals and a bride. Well done, ladies."

FLAME OF THE ROCKIES (SNEAK PEEK AT BOOK 6)

ANGELA BREIDENBACH

CHAPTER 1

4TH OF JULY 1910

Adair MT
Milwaukee Railroad Western Extension of the Idaho-Montana Border

Juliana Hayes squinted against the sun breaking over the sharp rock outline of the Bitterroot Mountains. Each escaping ray ratcheted up the thermometer in the early Pacific Northwest morning. Giant cedars looming above eighty-foot white pine should offer refuge and shade. Instead they represented the immobile bars of her prison.

In the distance, the forest closed so tightly it looked like rolls of dark green velvet. Such beauty hiding the malevolent nature of the area's extreme dangers. As dangerous as some of the men Juliana cautiously avoided since being stranded.

How much longer until she could break out of the harsh existence that held her captive for over two years? The deep snows in winter and the fires in summer, extremes she could do without. The oncoming train puffed out clouds of smoke against the sky so blue and clear it resembled a lake more than the heavens. But she'd ridden that train many times praying they'd make it to the next mining camp through heavy snow and bitter cold. Did there exist another place so wildly inhospitable?

"Anot'er hot day, Mrs. Hayes." The baggage handler lifted his flat cloth cap and rubbed a gray cotton sleeve across his forehead. "Who knew America would be such a hot place?" He flopped the cap back on his head as he waited with her on Adair's platform for the train to sidle up. She'd join the shift change for the mines dotted through the wilderness settlements and narrow, serpentine valley to deliver her quota of baked goods.

"We've never had a summer as hot before, not that I can remember." Was he Austrian, Belgian, Croatian? She didn't ask. He obviously wasn't Chinese or Japanese with his blond hair. She tried not to wrinkle her nose. It was blond, wasn't it? Hard to tell when these men likely bathed only on their day off. He stood tall enough to stick out among the Japanese who mostly inhabited the tent city of Adair nowadays. "After the avalanches in the spring, I don't think anyone expected this drought."

"I heard da winters here are hard. You do good wi' dem?"

She nodded, avoiding too much conversation. There must be more than seventy different nationalities working on the rails and the mines here on the border of Montana and Idaho. Some nationalities so close they spoke similar languages, only the colors or sometimes a piece of native clothing distinguished them one from another. This mishmash of humanity from every known continent all with the same hope—to make their fortunes, whether to bring over more family or get rich quick or hide from the law. Money drove these desperate men.

His clothing suggested another Austrian. They tended to band together, each of these different nationalities. It helped with communication overall as the foremen spoke English and the native language of their crews, sometimes a few more. The mixed-pigeon varieties were endless, and sometimes humorous, but the pigeon languages helped bridge one group to another unless they clashed. They often clashed. Tempers as hot as the rail spikes in the sun after a day of excruciating cold, wet work deep in the rocky mountainsides. As important the sense of togetherness inside a group, ironic how that togetherness habitually incited aggression and animosity toward outsiders. Why couldn't they all just get along?

Juliana did her best to be as neutral and invisible as possible down to wearing dull clothing and keeping her long hair tied up under her baker's scarf. But as a young woman, that worked as well as a queen bee in a hive. She hated developing the stinger that went along with the unwanted attention buzzing around her like soldier bees. But she'd been left with little other protection when her husband died.

Not long now. She calculated her time left based on her weekly pay envelope. She could shed the protective veneer in nine weeks, six days, and twelve hours—give or take the time it took to leave the mountains behind. She'd have her trunk on the very next train to Helena without a second glance. There'd be no salt pillar of Juliana Hayes in Adair, Idaho or any other debauched mining town in this forsaken place.

This Austrian, or whatever, was new on the job in a constantly changing mass of men. He'd met her at the brick dome ovens in Adair the last few days to help load a converted mining cart with the staples she baked for the workers up and down the line. At least she could understand his English— and he didn't seem to be a Montenegrin by the look of him. Those vicious men tended to work in Rowland and Taft, on her Tuesday and least favorite route. Why did she have to feed the very men who murdered her husband? A shiver ran through her spine. She'd have to deliver the bread order tomorrow. Each week she considered adding sawdust, or worse, to the dough—and each week she mashed the desire down deep as she punched the bread into submission. Twenty loaves untainted by her dark desire for vengeance. *Vengeance is mine, saith the Lord.* She repeated that verse each time the snake's temptation squeezed its coils around her heart.

"I hear said da snow gets deep as the depot roof."

Juliana nodded again and graced the man with a quick, courteous smile careful not to encourage anything. Too nice a response would garner yet another proposal or a lewd proposition. No response and she'd have to lug all four heavy freight baskets onto the train to the next stop on her daily deliveries. Her pay packet from the railroad would be reduced if she cost precious production minutes, she knew from experience when she first started for the Milwaukee Railroad. The company didn't care that she was a new widow. They cared she kept up with her quotas.

"Too bad we don't have a little snow left over." She mumbled as pleasant as possible, under the circumstances. "I hope we don't see a fire season so dangerous again as that one two years ago." She didn't want to relive a summer like that for more reasons than the spot wildfires. Her grief had been as thick as the smoke trapped by the jagged peaks.

"Was bad, ja?"

"Yes."

The engine whistle blew three long shrieks as metal on metal squealed a high-pitched complaint braking the train to a stop. The nearness of the rocky mountain slopes amplified the sounds. The conductor, in overalls and brimmed summer hat, leaned out the caboose porch. He leapt onto the wooden platform and ran nimbly along the train before it had a chance to stop, bellowing, "All 'board! Let's be movin', folks." He inspected the waiting cargo, including the amount Juliana brought aboard. "Mornin', Widow Hayes."

"Good morning, Mr. Kelly." She handed him a couple of buttermilk biscuits filled with apple butter wrapped in cheesecloth. The conductor often missed meals for train delays. "There's one for the engineer also."

"Yer a good woman, ya are." He tipped his hat and strode at a fast pace toward the front. "Johnnie, we been visited by the Angel of Adair! Looky the size of them biscuits!" Only he called her that and only he was allowed. The older man, stronger than his wrinkles led one to believe, had shoved more than his share of miscreants off the train for inter-fering in her duties.

Johnnie Mackedon tooted out his thanks on the whistle. One of his signatures. Stay long enough and each engineer could be recognized by the way they pulled the train whistle.

She laughed and gave him a quick wave as she called out, "You're welcome, Johnnie."

The burly handler lifted the heavier basket laden with oversized loaves and walked with Juliana toward the steps leading into the first passenger car.

As he shifted to pass another up to the top step, he said, "Mizz Hayes, I been meanin'—"

Juliana made a show of focusing on raising her skirt to climb the steps. Three days it took him. Must be a record. "Oh look, the front seats are open. Mr. Kelly keeps them clear for me, you know." Prime space to settle in with her tasty cargo that still wafted the fresh-baked aroma of oat bran, whole wheat, and honey all around her. The rich scent of baked goods helped to mask the constant smell of the muck of the mines. She always rode in front. First on and off to keep deliveries moving, and the unwanted scent of unwashed bodies blown behind her by the open windows. In the front, she avoided eye contact. They might approach her with odious offers, but none would dare take a Milwaukee Railroad baker's chosen space. The company provided the best grub in the country for their workforce, supplementing the regular camp cooks. Bellies held priority until full. Then it switched to other appetites. Appetites she refused to fill.

All eyes devoured her as if she were a Sunday cinnamon raisin bun. How unfriendly did she have to be to protect herself? It seemed the colder she behaved the harder some men tried. She'd heard the dares and the bets and chose to ignore them. One at a time, she could rebuff the advances.

"Mizz—"

"I don't want to keep you from your other freight or we'll both get docked for delaying the shift change." Not today. She didn't want to be targeted by teeming crews snatching up the handful of women as wives or worse. No, she couldn't stomach it today of all days. She lifted the nearest bread crate and stowed it.

"Ma'am, the party tonight, if you're of the mind —" His voice soft, pleading.

He might even be a nice man. But Juliana didn't want a man here, nice or otherwise. She took the last crate from him and backed away, setting the bread on the front seat beside her. The length hung well beyond the edge. With those stacked on the floor near her feet, another across the aisle, they formed a sort of protective fencing. A small fortress protecting her personal space.

The whistle blew, sounding departure. She couldn't give him a hair of a chance to spit the rest of the words out. "I'll bring a few loaves of hearty dark rye in the morning. I know that's a favorite with the wild onion and venison sandwiches. I heard your bunkhouse got a big buck the other day.

Maybe a trade for some meat?" The extra work would be worth it if she could supplement her pantry and not spend out of her savings. And steer the conversation away from what she knew came next.

"Good, ja, to be sure. Would you—"

The conductor pushed through the entry. "Get on back to loading, Jack." He jabbed an elbow into the baggage man's ribs, whose name was something more like Jacques, if one could get the accent right. "The Widow Hayes got 'er job and yous got yers. Move it, man, get those supplies loaded and leave room for them pack horses!"

A moment later, Juliana escaped the first proposal of the day by luck and by golly. At least he'd tried to be nice. Three stops to dispatch last night's labor, and a basket of buttermilk biscuits for the highest weekly production, then the ride back to Adair. Tomorrow she'd deliver to Rowland and the cycle would continue six days out of seven. The Rowland baker from down the line would overlap schedules for her one day off on Sunday, as the others did for the all the mining camps stretched through the long valley along the tracks. Juliana rarely saw the other women as they worked each other's days off. Most had marital and family duties to catch up. Each baked for her camp and three to four more that either didn't have an oven and baker or she only worked part-time due to other responsibilities.

She slid against the seatback savoring the air flowing in from the window. So many days lately the air stood still as a deer at the crack of a twig. Her only relief came from the train window. Juliana split her schedule and baked half her quota well before dawn during the summer to avoid the intense heat of the huge brick ovens in the late afternoon, the hottest part of the day in the Idaho panhandle.

She had little chance of avoiding several more marriage—or unmentionable—invitations with the significance of the holiday for citizens and immigrants alike. She smoothed the worn white apron over her tan cotton work skirt. She'd have on black still, but that brought the men out of the tunnels and mines as much as the whiskey called them to the saloons. A black dress meant a woman had no man, fair game in this most beautiful of desolate places. Mary, a new baker, had been carried to the preacher within days of arriving last summer. Carried. That miner wasn't taking a chance of cold feet or bridal theft. Bridal theft could get a man killed in these parts as much as having the precious commodity of a bride, if she were particularly desirable. Most respected marriage, though they'd line up to pay respects at any married man's funeral in hopes of walking the new widow right past her home and into theirs. Women like Astrid picked a new husband quickly, especially if she had children to support. These mountains could be ruthless in weather and wild animals.

This summer poor Mary nursed a newborn and baked. Mary managed to give away one of her days to another miner's wife, a previous canary, that wanted honest work rather than the bawdy house her husband had found her in. *Not me, Lord. Be it your will, I'm getting out of here come end of September! I am not raising a family here, if you ever grace me with a good man again let it be in a city! Strike that. I'd rather just have a city life.*

Some days Juliana felt more like a lone stalk of grain in a herd of buffalo bulls all snorting and ramming one another. After this summer ended, she'd have enough to move on before the harsh winter hit again. She'd take this very train into Helena, Montana, the Queen City of the Rockies, and never look back. Maybe she'd continue to Minneapolis or keep going as far East as Chicago. With the mastery of mass baking she'd gained, her own pastry shop would serve cookies, cakes, and anything to break the monotony of wheat bread and sour dough, four days a week, cinnamon raisin or another sweet bread on Saturdays for their Sunday meals, and the dark rye to the weekly winners of extra rations.

Only a short ride between towns, the train wove beside the St. Joe river, flowing low from the heat and lack of rain, and around the wide bend before pulling into Kyle. Deliver into the depot, climb on the next train to Stetson. Deliver, climb on the next train to Avery. Then home to Adair to start the dough for tomorrow. The cycle didn't slow. Mix dough, bake bread, deliver bread to miners and railroaders. Keep them working. Juliana stared out the window at the white pine, cedar, and river flashing past as they rode deeper into the rugged realm. Why couldn't she have fallen in love with a man who would stay in the city the first time? She could have avoided this day when everyone else would celebrate the country's independence, it was the second anniversary of her husband's death.

"Get outta my way!" The shouts erupted several rows from the front.

"I got dibs!"

Juliana rolled her eyes heavenward, but didn't bother to look at the skirmish. She already knew what caused the fight. She plunked her elbow on the window ledge and dropped her chin into it, staring at the passing landscape. Nine weeks and six days...

CHAPTER 2

LUKAS TOOK a headcount of his newly hired crew
as they boarded the back of the railcar from the
Kyle platform. He breathed in relief as he followed
them inside. He'd pick up a few more extras from
the other foreman, if they had them, and head back
to Rowland. Better to be prepared for attrition.
Any given day a man walked off the job without a
word.

A whiff of fresh bread floated from the front of
the car, wafting in the air, between bodies pushing
for seating. He closed his eyes and inhaled deeply.
He'd like one good day this month. Just one. It'd be
topped off with a hunk of that bread and the ability
to concentrate on the actual job rather than
refilling empty positions for the company. His
stomach rumbled. Bad coffee reheated from last

night didn't make the best breakfast. Perhaps the baker would have a bite to spare in her bundles?

As the crowded aisle diminished, one lummox shoved another backward. "I ain't givin' way! She ain't got a man an' I ain't got a woman. I'm tired o' spendin' money on canaries."

"An' you ain't getting' betwixt she an' me!" The targeted victim, righted by his buddy behind him, used the upward momentum, and shoved back sending his opponent flying across two other men.

Shouts and curses turned to bets on the winner as the crew tossed the rivals in the middle.

"That don't make you the one she wants!"

In less time than the breadth of a horsehair, the first man fisted and decked the guy.

Not ducking out, the punched man recovered, again with the assistance of a buddy, and flew into battle. The rest of the crew leaned over seats, egging the two on, cheering for their favorite, and passing money to the man nearest the fight who acted as the bank.

By the time Lukas made it through the tangle of bodies blocking his progress, the culprits were on the floor trying to strangle one another over another woman. Not the first fight he'd seen since females were as rare in this rugged country as trout in the low river. The job challenged the strongest men physically, mentally, and spiritually. After a month as the hiring foreman, he'd discovered the most grueling job, his, was keeping the mines running against the constant loss of manpower from giving up or getting beat or moving on. Men could take the hard work. They could handle the extremes in temperature. But the lack of womankind wreaked havoc in a way he couldn't have fathomed when he agreed to the contract. Men forged the roads, built the towns, answered the call of adventure. But women—they tamed hearts, settled men, and created civilization.

The production reports took backseat to order, discipline, and the act of production. Two months of reports from the last foreman never happened. Now he knew why. His first had yet to be finished for the company. But if he lost any more men, he'd be down in the mines working an empty shift again. Though he'd earned respect by doing it. Now this mess—before the day even started—he pushed the gawkers in the inner circle back into their seats, a firm hand on a shoulder if one protested. They took one look at who dared and backed down. Many here stood taller than average and sported physiques built out of years on farms, railroads, mines, or prison. All came for the opportunity, but few boasted the equivalent of his height and frame. The epitome of a European man who'd worked hard through his boyhood. That fact alone stopped many problems. He had the additional benefit of an excellent education and leadership skills. Then his deep voice cinched it for the rest.

Lukas grabbed a handful of shirt collar and

hauled the bigger brute up in one yank. The man landed on his feet staring up into his foreman's darkened glare. "You will stop." The other contender leapt to his feet and launched forward, fists primed. Lukas extended a flat palm with such force toward the oncoming attacker, he knocked the wind out of him. "You will also stop."

Never once did he raise his voice above a low growl as he spoke in his native language. His height alone commanded attention. But accompanied by the muscular body of heavy labor since childhood cowed most would-be challengers. Add the resonant baritone, that when raised in worship filled a church with beauty song. That same vocal quality, directed in discipline, shook the recipient to the core. As head foreman, in charge of men pushed past human endurance, decency in the ranks didn't last long. Lukas had no choice but to be half father and half bouncer. What he couldn't afford to be was too close of a friend, not among these intense conditions. Enough to build connection and enough command to build respect. Something his father had taught him about managing their holdings while tutoring Lukas to take over.

"What was this about?" He asked the man whose scruff he still held.

"Her." He pointed at the baker in the front row, wooden bins of bread all around her making a kind of blockade. She faced forward with a stiffened spine, pointedly ignoring the scene not far behind her, arms wrapped tightly around her torso. Did she know the fight was over her or couldn't she understand the language?

One of the miners nearby laughed, and explained, "Ain't no big deal. Someone's always makin' a play for her. She ain't givin' the likes o' those two no never mind. Gotta be a rich man to catch a gal like that one. I'll get me rich and then get that gal for my personal canary." The fellows around him slapped him on the back. "You'll all be jealous then."

The bakers, hired directly by the Milwaukee Railroad, were hard to find and a difficult position to refill. If Lukas wanted bread for his crews, that lady needed protection from the men she had to feed.

He switched to English hoping the woman would understand he had everything under control. "You will all leave the baker alone. If not, you will answer to me." He narrowed his eyes, looked at each man, and asked, "Do we understand each other?"

Lukas caught a flicker of movement in the front row. Had she glanced over her shoulder?

"Ja." The one who could speak said as he nodded.

Letting the man go, he pointed at the bench several rows back. Then he turned to the smaller culprit. "Und?"

He nodded.

Lukas released him.

The fellow sputtered, wheezed, and worked his way down the aisle doubled-over to sit as far away from Lukas as he could get.

Lukas stared down the entire compartment. Then he shook his head. One perfect day. This wouldn't be it. He searched for a seat, catching hold of one he passed to balance as the train swayed around a bend. All full until he reached the front.

"May I?" He asked the pretty bread baker. The company of a sweet soul with kind words would do a lot to ease the stress today.

She turned from the window, sized him up with caramel brown eyes in a flash that rocked him as hard as dynamite blasting a mining shaft. "No."

IF YOU'D LIKE TO CONTINUE READING *FLAME of theRockies*, please visit AngelaBreidenbach.com or your favorite bookstore.

MONTANA TRAVEL TIPS

Welcome to your fifth installment in our Montana Travel Tips. This is our first story in the 6-book series that goes outside the borders of Montana. Since we travel with our brilliant Montana women to Chicago's White City, built specifically to house the 1893 World's Fair celebrating the 500th anniversary of the discovery of the Americas, we're going to explore travel to and from this beautiful state and the various options for transportation in the fourth largest state in the US. I think you'll find a few surprises you won't want to miss!

Top cross-border travel includes air, train, roads, snow sports, water, horseback. Let's take a look at each one to find your perfect travel option(s). You might do what our family has done and combine several. Why not? Makes for a unique vacation to see how many different modes of transportation you can take—no rules, count them all. Don't forget to make a memory album because your family will want to remember it! Our family still talks about our vacation based on how many transportation options we could find.

By Air: We have a few main cities for airlines including Billings, Bozeman, Butte, Great Falls, Kalispell, and Missoula (waving at you). These six small cities are served by major airlines. But a few of those airlines only operate in our cities during the warmer weather. So check for better seats and competition a few months before coming in the summer. There are also several small airports, but they're usually commuter or private planes. Curious? Here's a Wikipedia list complete with how many passengers "enplane" at those locations. https://en.wikipedia.org/wiki/List_of_airports_in_Montana

Seats sell out pretty quickly because quite a few are smaller planes (puddle jumpers). Alaska, Allegiant, Delta, and United tend to be year-round. We've had some ping pong in and out over the years including Frontier and American. Some airlines service more flights to Bozeman for ski season. Additionally, we have a tiny commuter airline, Cape Air **https://www.capeair.com/where_we_fly/Montana/montana.html**, that goes to the High Line area. A must visit is the underground city tour in Havre, MT! You'd fly to Billings and then catch a Cape Air flight for a song.

That tour is unbelievable! One of my favorite underground tours ever, and I find them wherever I go! **https://havrechamber.com/explore/bear-paw-ski-bowl-2** Havre's tour tops Seattle's underground tour in my book.

Another little-known service are our private pilots that volunteer for Angel Wings West carrying specialty health passengers to care inside and outside of Montana.

Plan for connections. Unless you're coming straight from Denver, Las Vegas, Minneapolis, Phoenix, Los Angeles, Salt Lake, or Seattle you're not likely to find a direct flight. Well, not as of this writing. But, things never stay the same … the Missoula International Airport is currently expanding (2021). Maybe the makeshift Gate 7 that winds through the restaurant will become a real gate in the new wing. It could happen.

If you're traveling around the Pacific Northwest, you can find better air fares into Spokane. But that's a three-hour drive from Missoula in good weather. We try to avoid going over the major passes during cold weather. They're quite treacherous even with ice tires. Yes, ice tires. I don't do winter without them!

Let's talk driving to and from Montana. Getting on the road is a wonderful way to slow down and enjoy the vistas. Coming from the south, up I-15, we stop in Beaver, UT for the Cache Valley Dairy. Our family places cheese orders in the hundreds of dollars. Breaks up a really long drive between Las Vegas and Missoula at a beautiful travel stop for lunch and stocking up on cheese curds. Beware the weather on that stretch as well as the Monida Pass. Blizzards are common October through April. The same is true of Lookout Pass coming from the western border of Montana and Idaho. Yes, Idaho borders Montana on two sides.

Heading from Montana down through Wyoming to Denver is both gorgeous and can be treacherous in winter. I've been stuck in a white out there, too, in March. But the summer drives all around are majestic.

Going east to North Dakota, you may have a long view of the Norther Lights. We did one late summer drive. Those green glowing sky dances lasted for hours. I'll never forget it!

Now, heading north to Canada you'll have some Great Plains options or a short window in the summer to experience the top of the world on the Going to the Sun Highway through Glacier Park. On any of these amazing drives, summer preferred, get out and hike. Breathe the air and feast on the gorgeous views.

No matter which way you come from, the roads are long. Be sure to check your gas tank and know where your fuel stops will be located. My favorite way to do that is with the app Gas Buddy. I can check prices and play the silly game of getting nonsense points for loading prices for other drivers. You don't really get anything for the points, but you can enter drawings for free gas with them. Nope, I've never won anything. But it does entertain me in the lowest level as a passenger.

My favorite way to entertain myself and family on long road trips? Audiobooks! One of my goals with the Queen of the Rockies series is to get all six books into an audiobook series. But that takes a lot of money to set up. So let's hope a lot of books sell to make it possible. Otherwise, tune into the various podcasts you'll find on my website including Genealogy Publishing Coach. Or listen to your favorite audiobooks and let us all know your favs!

Waterways are full of rafting, boating, and memories of grand paddle boats that cruised up the Missouri. Boating is a very popular hobby in Montana. Just be sure to check the laws if you're pulling a boat across state lines to get checked for invasive mussels or other species not allowed.

Can you really ride a horse? You bet. Just plan for a really, really, really long ride as Montana is about 600 miles across. Quite a few small outfits exist for hunting, riding, and dude ranching with guided horse tours, camping, and wilderness experiences.

You might prefer the train across the High Line (up by Canada) or an RV with camping. Motorcycles cruise all over the back roads and highways.

Amtrak does come through the northern parts of Montana. Though there's a lot of talk and work happening for a revival of a passenger train line that would go through the lower half of the state. I have dreams of that in the future. One day I hope to ride a sleeper car across America from Missoula. Amtrak does have a residency for writers. They range from short to long and are by application. Wouldn't that be an experience?

Last but not least, snow sports like skiing and snowmobiling can cross the Montana borders because some of the snowy play areas are literally on the Idaho Montana border. In book 6, *Flame of the Rockies*, we're going to visit the western border where the largest fire in US history burned in 1910. The train and mining history there is incredible. I can't wait to share it with you in that story and introduce you to some true heroes (and some black sheep) that made the Trail of the Hiawatha vibrant!

Regardless of how you choose to travel to Montana, please come visit. You'll love it here!

As I travel around the world, and Montana, I sometimes put reviews up on TripAdvisor and Google Maps. Both spots you can find me via @AngBreidenbach like all my social media. I give honest reviews and try to include photos as well as gluten-free spots when I find them.

Travel blessings,

Angela Breidenbach

I hope you enjoyed *Bride of the Rockies*, book 5 in the Queen of the Rockies series. I loved sharing a little-known true Montana history about how our women became famous around the world. Little-known history easily becomes lost history. By sharing stories like this, we won't let it be forgotten.

I wrote six stories that tell some of the special events and what happens as Montana becomes a state in the Queen of the Rockies Series. The next books in the series will complete the set. *Flame of the Rockies* is about the largest fire in US History that happened on the western border of Idaho-Montana in the rough, ramshackle mining and train towns of the mountain wilderness. All six are available in e-book, paperback, and large print editions.

As an author, I love feedback. Candidly, you're the reason I continue to explore the history of Montana. So tell me what you liked or loved, what questions or thoughts this book brought to mind, or what made you laugh and cry. You can write to me on the contact page of my website. I do answer emails personally. Visit me on the web at: http://AngelaBreidenbach.com or tune into one of my podcasts also easily found on my site. I hope you'll enjoy reading the stories I write and listening to my shows and interviews.

Finally, please consider writing a review for this book. Reviews help books sell and keep writers writing. Would you kindly leave a review on your favorite site such as Bookbub, Goodreads, Amazon, or any other review site? Your feedback is important to me and very appreciated! Reviews can be hard to come by these days. You, the reader, have the power now to make or break a book.

Thank you so much for reading *Bride of the Rockies*, spending time with the people of Montana, and I hope you'll also enjoy the sample chapter of *Flame of the Rockies*, the last of this series. You'll find it at the end of this story. But most of all, thank you for spending time with me. I'll see you in the pages of the next book.

If you'd like to receive new release information, genealogy tips, or keep up with me through my newsletter please consider signing up when you visit my website or you can join at this link: https://landing.mailerlite.com/webforms/ landing/n0s2t2
Appreciatively,
Angela Breidenbach

P.S. Here's a little about the other books in the first few years of Montana's statehood:

Did you miss the beginning of Frankie and Joey's story in Queen of the Rockies?
What if you were caught doing something good, but the man you loved didn't see it that way? Meet Calista Blythe and Albert Shanahan in 1889...

Queen of the Rockies, Book 1 and kick off title of the series by Angela Breidenbach ~ 1889 (Helena, MT): Calista Blythe enters the first Miss Snowflake Pageant celebrating Montana statehood to expose the plight of street urchins. But hiding an indentured orphan could unravel Calista's reputation, and her budding romance with pageant organizer, Albert Shanahan, if her secret is revealed. Will love or law prevail?

Song of the Rockies. 1890 Montana historical.
What would you do if you were given eleven

rowdy street newsies and told either you turn them into model citizens or they get sold into indenture or sent to the military? **Song of the Rockies** is the story of a sweet music teacher, Mirielle Sheehan, and eleven boys given one chance or else! Evan Russell lost everything—his ranch, his wife, and now after trusting relatives with his young son, even the little boy is missing. How can a beautiful symphony of the heart come from such chaos? *Reminiscent of Little Men.*

Heart of the Rockies. 1892 Montana historical.

Could she believe in herself when no one else did?

A progressive thinker in 1892 Montana, Delphina O'Connor believed in God-given dreams for women didn't stop at marriage and children. Hers might not include a husband or family at all. So when Hugh Thomas rescues the new swimming instructor at the elegant Broadwater Natatorium from near drowning in the plunge, how can anyone believe the freedom to enjoy swimming, competition, and a healthy body is an appropriate activity for a proper lady? Hugh is about to find out status quo is the starting line for a courageous woman with a dream!

Heart of the Rockies explores the real-world question: What do you do when you think differently than the world around you?

Flower of the Rockies. 1892-1895 Montana historical.

Can you leave your past behind?

No one knows the real Emmalee Warren, or the sacrifices she's made for love. An infamous soiled dove of no consequence turned miner's widow. Men are coming out of the woodwork to stake their claim on her and the mine she inherited. They wanted her body before. Now they want her money, and they'll do anything to take it. But love and acceptance seem out of the question for Emmalee.

Society wants nothing to do with her regardless of her changed ways. Who can she turn to when her inheritance and chance at a future is at risk? Will she be forced back into the brothel to survive? Hiring a lawyer, Richard Lewis, to save her from financial ruin might let her start over somewhere else — if he can save a little of her finances from her husband's partner. She'll go anyplace else where no one knows Miss Ellie's name. Anywhere to leave the scorn behind. Becoming an unknown is the only way to freedom...or is it? Can she leave her past and build a new future?

Bride of the Rockies. 1893 Montana Historical

Would she give up her dream for love?

For botanist, Bettina Gilbert, mining is an offense against God's green earth. With the shortage of women in Montana, Luke travels to

Chicago to manage the Montana mining exhibition hoping to also find a wife. Only that pretty botanist keeps disrupting his mining presentations … and his chances of meeting the right woman! A city girl who despises his way of life would be the worst choice for a miner's wife, wouldn't she?

Flame of the Rockies. 1910 Montana Historical
Can she release her prejudice to love again?
August 1910, Idaho/Montana Border
The fiery pain at her new husband's murder might equal the disaster blazing across the Pacific Northwest. Stranded in the treacherous railroad camp, baking bread for survival, Juliana Hayes has no desire to marry a railroad ruffian like Lukas Filips, or anyone else. Can she release her prejudice to love again? Or will either one of them survive The Big Blowup to find out?

Based on true history when three million acres burned out of control on the border of Montana and Idaho darkening the skies all the way to the East Coast. It's a wonder anyone survived!

ALSO BY ANGELA BREIDENBACH

Queen of the Rockies

Song of the Rockies

Heart of the Rockies

Flower of the Rockies

Bride of the Rockies

Flame of the Rockies

Other Fiction:

The Mail-Order Standoff

A Healing Heart

Nonfiction:

Gems of Wisdom — The Treasure of Experience

Find more books at AngelaBreidenbach.com or your favorite store.

ABOUT THE AUTHOR

 Angela Breidenbach is a professional genealogist, media personality, bestselling author, and screenwriter. She's also the Christian Authors Network president. Angie lives in Montana with her hubby and Muse, a trained fe-lion, who shakes hands, rolls over, and jumps through a hoop. Surprisingly, Angie can also. Catch her show and podcast, Genealogy Publishing Coach!

http://AngelaBreidenbach.com
A-Muse-ings Newsletter for new releases, genealogy tips, fascinating history, and fun events:
https://landing.mailerlite.com/webforms/landing/n0s2t2
Social Media: @AngBreidenbach

facebook.com/angbreidenbach

twitter.com/angbreidenbach

instagram.com/angbreidenbach

amazon.com/Angela-
Breidenbach/e/B00460W4F4

goodreads.com/AngBreidenbach

pinterest.com/angbreidenbach